Once Upon a Time on 9/11

Once Upon a Time on 9/11

— A ROLLIE FINCH MYSTERY —

AL LAMANDA

Encircle Publications
Farmington, Maine, U.S.A.

Once Upon a Time on 9/11 Copyright © 2021 Al Lamanda

Paperback ISBN-13: 978-1-64599-215-8
Hardcover ISBN-13: 978-1-64599-218-9
E-book ISBN-13: 978-1-64599-216-5
Kindle ISBN-13: 978-1-64599-217-2

Editor: Michael Piekny
Cover design: Christopher Wait
Cover images © Getty Images

Published by:

Encircle Publications
PO Box 187
Farmington, ME 04938

Visit: http://encirclepub.com
info@ encirclepub.com

Printed in U.S.A.

For those who lost their lives on 9/11.

PROLOGUE

New York City made Joanna Kearns sick.

When her plane landed at LaGuardia and she entered the terminal, it was so bad that she ran into the nearest bathroom and vomited. Afterward, she washed her face, brushed her hair, and inspected herself in the mirror. She looked fifty-nine, instead of her actual forty-nine.

When she felt well enough, she went to baggage claim for her lone suitcase and wheeled it curbside.

The air was hot and smelled of cab and bus fumes, neither of which helped her nausea.

A great deal had changed since she was last at LaGuardia. She found out, after wasting twenty minutes, that all the cab-spots on the street were reserved for Uber. She had to return to the terminal and take an elevator up two floors to get to the street level on the opposite side that was reserved for yellow cabs.

She waited in a very long line until it was her turn and discovered another change in that the fare was a flat rate to Manhattan. The ride to her hotel on 53rd and Broadway, a distance of less than ten miles, took an hour and fifteen minutes, thanks to traffic.

She used the time to read her notes and rehearse what she was going to tell the police so that she didn't sound like a babbling hysteric.

When she finally reached the hotel and checked in, the first thing she did was take a long, hot shower to wash the sweat of traveling off her body.

Refreshed and changed, Joanna took up her handbag and left the hotel. She told the driver to take her to the 23rd Precinct on East 102nd Street.

The neighborhood and police station hadn't changed much since she moved away from the city. The police station was old and needed paint. The lobby was filled with uniformed officers. She went up to the desk sergeant.

"May I help you, miss?" he said.

"Yes. The last time I was here I spoke with Detective Timmons," Joanna said. "I wonder where I might find him."

"Detective Timmons retired a long time ago," the sergeant said. "Is there something I can help you with?"

"Maybe I can see another detective?" Joanna said. "I've come a very long way."

"I'll call the squad room and see who is available," the sergeant said.

A few moments later, Joanna was escorted through the detective's squad room to the desk of Detective Joe Chiles. Chiles was a handsome Black man of about forty, with bright, clear eyes and a soft voice.

"Miss…?" he said.

"Joanna Kearns."

"How can I help you, Miss Kearns?" Chiles said.

"The last time I was here, I spoke with Detective Timmons about my sister's murder," Joanna said. "I was hoping to talk to him again."

"Detective Timmons retired," Chiles said.

"So I was told."

"When was your sister murdered?" Chiles said.

"On September 11th," Joanna said.

"So, about six months ago?"

Joann shook her head. "No, in 2001," she said.

CHAPTER ONE

Rollie Finch always enjoyed making breakfast for his three daughters. Today he made Spanish omelets and toast, served with orange juice.

Grace was oldest at 17, followed by Giselle at 15, and Gloria, the youngest, barely a teenager at 13.

All three were spitting images of their mother, Georgia, who died three years ago. They all had her spirit and independence.

"Dad, when are you going to get a new car?" Grace said.

Rollie owned an old LeSabre.

"What's wrong with the Buick?" Rollie said as he served the omelets.

"It's not cool," Gloria said.

"Oh, I'm sorry," Rollie said. "I didn't realize a car needed to be cool in order for it to go from point A to point B."

"We need to go to the mall," Grace said. "It's embarrassing being seen getting out of an old man's car."

"Why do you need to go to the mall?" Rollie said.

"We need back to school clothes," Giselle said. "You can't expect us to wear last year's clothes."

"Heaven forbid," Rollie said.

There came cries of 'Dad, get real' and 'Do you want us to be embarrassed?' and their sky seemed to be falling.

Rollie sighed. "How much do you need?" he said.

"We don't know until we see what they have," Grace, the oldest, said.

"What about school supplies?" Rollie said.

"What school supplies?" Grace said. "This isn't the one room schoolhouse like when you went to school, Dad."

Rollie sighed, defeated in the eyes of the enemy. "You three do the dishes and tidy up the kitchen, and then you can go to the mall."

"You always give in," said Gloria, the youngest.

"I want to see everything you buy," Rollie said. "Including receipts."

"Of course," Grace said.

After breakfast, while the girls tidied up the kitchen, Rollie went to his office, which was in the garage. Originally built as a three-car garage, Rollie installed a wall that cut the garage space down to hold one-car, and made a comfortable, working office for himself after he retired from the NYPD.

At five-foot-nine inches tall and a solid one-hundred-and-eighty pounds, Rollie could still fit into his rookie uniform, thanks mostly to hour-long workouts on the step-climber in the rear of his garage.

His sandy-colored hair was speckled with grey, but his blue eyes still had remnants of his youth in them, even though he turned forty-eight just three months ago.

Armed with a large mug of coffee, Rollie took a seat at his desk and used the remote to open the garage door and allow sunshine and fresh air into the office.

He had three very lengthy reports to type up and he got right to work on his old computer.

At eighteen, Rollie had joined the Army, as had his father and grandfather. While at Fort Bragg, he took college night classes and the exam for the New York City Police Department and was called shortly before his discharge.

By his twenty-second birthday, Rollie was a rookie cop assigned to a fourteen-year-veteran training officer.

Showing a real aptitude for police work, Rollie made detective by age thirty, homicide by age thirty-two, and lieutenant by age thirty-five.

A year after he joined the department, he married Georgia, his high school sweetheart. They lived in a basement apartment in Long Island City rather than with either of their parents. She was a teacher and, at first, things were tight financially. After a few years of skimping and saving, they were able to put a down payment on a small home in the Queens neighborhood called Roosevelt.

They tried for a child. Georgia had two miscarriages, and they took some time off from trying to conceive.

The year that Rollie made detective, Georgia became pregnant again and this time she gave birth. Two years later, when Rollie made homicide, their second child was born.

They knew they needed a larger home. They sold the starter house and used the money to buy the home with four bedrooms and three bathrooms in Kew Gardens that he and the girls still occupied.

The year Rollie made lieutenant, their third child was born.

A lieutenant's pay was decent money, but Georgia insisted upon returning to work because she loved teaching, and the extra money provided a nice cushion.

She taught for eight more years until the cancer showed up in a routine exam, and three years later, she was gone.

Rollie retired from the department to take care of her. There were some good days, but they became fewer in number and finally there were none.

Georgia died peacefully at home in her own bed, surrounded by Rollie and the girls.

There was some insurance money, and his pension for twenty-three years on the job was good but not great, and he had three daughters to raise and send to college.

His old partner, Bill Teal, suggested Rollie apply for a private investigator's license. Law firms always needed good investigators, Teal said, and he proved to be correct.

From the start, Rollie discovered that the services of a highly qualified investigator were invaluable to law firms throughout the city. He accepted only criminal assignments and wanted nothing to do with divorce attorneys or ambulance chasers. By the second year, his income from private investigations doubled that of his pension.

The girls entered the garage through the connecting door.

"Kitchen's clean, Dad," Grace said. "We're going to the mall now."

"Which one?"

"Valley Stream is closest," Grace said.

Rollie stood and went to the back of the garage to open the safe. He used the keypad mounted to the safe to turn off the alarm and then entered the seven digit code and key to unlock it.

The safe contained two shotguns, a shelf full of ammunition, a .357 Magnum hand gun, and a cash box that held five thousand dollars in emergency funds. Rollie removed one thousand in twenties and returned to his desk.

He opened a drawer and pulled out a money belt and put the cash into the belt and gave it to Grace.

"Dad?" Grace said.

"Don't 'dad' me," Rollie said. "You wear this or you don't go."

Reluctantly, Grace took the belt, lifted her shirt and put the belt on. "Happy now?" she said.

"Yes," Rollie said and handed her the car keys. "Do you have your phones?"

All three girls turned to show Rollie their phones tucked into the back pocket of their jeans.

"What time should I expect you?" Rollie said.

"Five," Grace said. "Ish."

"What about lunch money?" Giselle said. "If we spend it from our new clothes money, we…"

Rollie removed his wallet and took out three twenty dollar bills and gave them to Grace.

"Thank you, Daddy," Grace said.

"Drive safe," Rollie said.

The girls opened the connecting door to the garage where the car was parked and closed it behind them.

He watched as Grace drove the Buick out of the garage and made a right turn.

"Okay," he said to himself and returned to work.

Around one o'clock, finished with the first report and halfway through the second, Rollie took a break to return to the kitchen to make a turkey sandwich with a glass of milk.

He returned to his desk and worked as he ate.

When the second report was complete, Rollie went to his bedroom and put on a teal colored warm-up suit and walking shoes and then returned to his office. He turned on sports radio, went to the step-climber for a one-hour workout.

After the workout, Rollie poured a tall glass of juice in the kitchen and then returned to work. He finished the third report by 4:30.

That's when his old friend and former partner Bill Teal called.

"Rollie, Bill," Teal said. "How's the gumshoe business?"

"Nobody says gumshoe anymore, Bill," Rollie said. "So, to what do I owe the honor?"

"There is a woman in my office," Teal said.

"I won't tell your wife if you don't," Rollie said.

Teal ignored the crack. "I'm sending her to see you because I can't help her with her problem."

"Which is?"

"It's better if she explains it," Teal said.

"Why can't you help her?" Rollie said.

"Manpower," Teal said. "You know how it is."

"Yeah, I know how it is," Rollie said. "When can I expect her?"

"Tomorrow morning okay?" Teal said.

Rollie sighed.

"Thanks, Rollie, I owe you one," Teal said.

"You owe me many, is what you owe me," Rollie said and hung up.

•   •   •

Rollie was putting a roast in the oven for dinner when the girls arrived home. Each carried several large shopping bags that they brought to their rooms.

"You're late," Rollie said when the girls entered the kitchen.

"Ten minutes," Grace said. "Traffic."

Over the sink, Rollie started peeling potatoes and carrots. "So what did you buy?" he said.

"Nothing slutty," Grace said.

"Show me," Rollie said.

"Come on, girls," Grace said.

While Rollie chopped potatoes and carrots for the roast, Grace, Giselle, and Gloria put on a fashion show in the kitchen.

"Gloria, when did you grow…?" Rollie said.

"When she turned twelve, Dad," Grace said. "Like, a year ago."

"I see," Rollie said.

"We brought back change," Grace said.

"Really? How much?"

"Sixty dollars," Grace said. "We thought we'd use it to go see a movie tomorrow."

"This sixty dollars is going into the college fund," Rollie said.

A little while later, as they sat down to dinner, the phone rang. The closest was the wall phone in the kitchen and Grace scooped it up.

"Hello," Grace said.

She listened for a moment and then said, "Yes, he's here. Hold on."

Grace stretched the cord and handed the phone to Rollie.

"Rollie Finch here," he said.

"Mr. Finch, my name is Joanna Kearns," Joanna said. "I spoke with Captain Teal a while ago. He recommended you very highly."

"Yes, he called me," Rollie said.

"May I stop by tomorrow?" Joanna said. "It's important."

"What time?"

"Eleven o'clock okay?"

"Fine. Do you need directions?"

"Captain Teal wrote them down for me."

"I shall see you at eleven o'clock," Rollie said.

He stood and replaced the phone.

"She sounded very nice," Grace said. "Maybe she's pretty."

Rollie looked at his daughters. All three were grinning.

"Eat," he said.

CHAPTER TWO

Gloria kept watch at the front window in the living room while Giselle and Grace did the breakfast dishes. On Saturday, breakfast was more like brunch and they didn't eat until after ten.

At eleven o'clock, a yellow cab pulled into the driveway and a nice looking woman around her father's age got out and walked to the front door. She carried a large brief case in her right hand.

Gloria dashed into the kitchen.

"Dad's appointment is here and she's kinda hot for an older lady," she said.

"You guys make coffee. I'll show her in," Grace said.

As Grace walked to the front door, the bell rang. Grace reached the door and opened it.

"I'm… is this the Finch residence?" Joanna said.

"Yes. My dad is expecting you," Grace said. "Come in, he's in his office."

Joanna followed Grace to the door in the hallway between the living room and kitchen where she knocked once and opened the door.

"Dad, your appointment is here," Grace said.

After Joanna entered the garage office, Grace closed the door and rushed to the kitchen.

"Well?" Giselle said.

"She's around Dad's age and pretty attractive," Grace said.

"Is she Dad's type?" Giselle said.

"Who knows what Dad's type is, he married Mom right after high school," Grace said. "Is that coffee ready?"

"Yeah," Giselle said.

"I'll bring it to them," Grace said.

She filled a ceramic carafe with coffee, the creamer with milk, and placed them on a serving tray, along with mugs, sugar and spoons. "One of you squirts get the door," she said.

"I'll get it," Giselle said.

"Why you?" Gloria said.

"I'm older," Giselle said.

"I'm more adorable," Gloria said.

"Shut up the both of you and get the door," Grace said.

•   •   •

"Is that real tape in that recorder?" Joanna said as she watched Rollie load his tape recorder.

"Yes it is," Rollie said. "I record all business meetings and make notes later as I need them."

"How old is it?" Joanna said.

"It belonged to my father who was also a cop," Rollie said. "Okay, it's fully loaded, so let's begin."

There was a knock on the door, it opened and Rollie's three daughters walked in with a tray of coffee. "Freshly made," Grace said.

"My daughters," Rollie said as Grace set the tray on the desk. "Thank you, girls."

"You have beautiful daughters," Joanna said as the girls left the office and closed the door.

"They take after their mother in that regard," Rollie said. "She would have been proud of the way they're turning out."

"You're a widower?"

"Yes."

"I'm sorry."

"Thank you," Rollie said as he poured coffee. "Now, tell me why you're here."

Rollie switched the recorder on and sipped from his mug.

"I'm not sure where to begin," Joanna said.

"I find it best to take your time and tell me how I can help you. Anywhere is fine." Rollie said.

Joanna nodded, "My sister was murdered by her husband. I have no proof, but I know he killed her."

"When did this happen?" Rollie said.

"On September 11th," Joanna said.

"Of last year?" Rollie said.

"No, in 2001," Joanna said.

Rollie, about to take another sip, paused. "That's quite the date; almost twenty years ago," he said.

"But there is no limit on murder, is there?" Joanna said.

"No, but there is a limit as to what can be done with so old a case," Rollie said.

"That's what Captain Teal said," Joanna said.

"Tell me why you think your sister was murdered," Rollie said.

"My sister was very unhappy in her marriage," Joanna said. "She used to confide in me about her husband's affairs. She was going to divorce him. She told me that a few days before. On September 11th, we talked by phone at 8:15 in the morning and made plans to meet for lunch."

"Where did she work?" Rollie said.

"Tower One," Joanna said.

"I'm sorry," Rollie said.

"Mr. Finch, my sister was not in Tower One when it was struck by the plane," Joanna said. "Her apartment was on 101st Street and West End Avenue. There is no way she left her apartment after talking to me, walked to 96th Street to catch the subway to Chambers Street, and made it to her office on the 81st floor by the time that plane hit. No way."

Rollie nodded. It really wouldn't have been possible, he thought. "What was the phone call about that morning?"

"I can't say for sure," Joanna said. "All she said was she had something important to tell me and asked if we could meet for lunch."

"But you have your suspicions?"

"I think she was going to tell me she wanted a divorce," Joanna said.

"Okay, back up for a second," Rollie said. "The husband, was he home at the time of the call?"

"She didn't say, but I'm sure he was," Joanna said. "When I talked to Detective Timmons a few days later, he…"

"Detective Al Timmons?" Rollie said.

"Yes, do you know him?"

"Yes, please go on."

"John—that's Julia's husband—he told Detective Timmons that he was sick in bed on 9/11 and didn't know about the towers until he woke up around 11:30 when I called him. I called at least a dozen times prior to see if he had heard from Julia, but he didn't answer until 11:30."

"He slept through it?"

"That's what he told Detective Timmons."

"When did you inform Detective Timmons of your suspicions?" Rollie said.

"September 18th," Joanna said. "After the shock of losing my sister wore off a bit and I started to see things more clearly. I realized Julia could not have been in Tower One when the plane struck."

"Where were you living at the time?" Rollie said.

"With my husband on 96th and Second Avenue."

"That's why you went to the 23rd Precinct on 102nd Street?" Rollie said.

Joanna nodded.

"Can you remember what Detective Timmons told you?" Rollie said.

"I have copies of all his reports," Joanna said.

"I'll look at them in a bit, but first tell me what happened at the time," Rollie said.

Joanna nodded again. "I went to the police station and asked to see a detective," she said. "I was taken to see Detective Timmons and I told him my suspicions."

"And Detective Timmons did what?" Rollie said.

"He went to see John, my sister's husband," Joanna said. "Then he asked me to come see him about a week later. He told me there wasn't sufficient evidence to get a search warrant of my sister's apartment based upon my phone call and theory."

"But you think otherwise?" Rollie said.

"I wouldn't be here if I didn't."

"Why now, after nearly 20 years?"

"Because John Knox is a murderer and he should not be allowed to become governor of New York," Joanna said.

"John Knox, the lieutenant governor?" Rollie said. "That's your former brother-in-law?"

"Yes," Joanna said. "And that monster can't be allowed to get away with it."

"Mrs. Kearns, there is no way on earth a district attorney would agree to indict John Knox on your say so," Rollie said.

"That's what Captain Teal said yesterday," Joanna said.

"And you don't believe him?" Rollie said.

"I wouldn't have come to you otherwise," Joanna said.

"No, I suppose not."

"Captain Teal said you were the best detective he's ever seen," Joanna said. "Can't you at least take a look for yourself and make your own decision?"

"Where do you live now, Mrs. Kearns?" Rollie said.

"South Carolina."

"How long will you be in New York?"

"Two more days."

"I'll give you until you go home to make a decision," Rollie said. "Leave me all your documents. They will be safe with me."

"Your fee," Joanna said. "I have no idea what any of this costs."

"My policy is never to break someone's bank," Rollie said. "My retainer is five thousand dollars. If I decide not to take the job I return it minus my time spent. If I do take the job the fee is seventy-five an hour plus expenses until the five thousand is used up and if you wish to continue, we negotiate. Are you in a position to afford that?"

"I still work. I'm a teacher like my sister was, and I have the insurance money from my husband; I can afford it," Joanna said.

"Okay. Fill out my retainer form and write a check, and I'll see what I see and report back to you," Rollie said.

"Thank you," Joanna said.

There was a soft knock on the door and it opened and Gloria stepped in to do the dirty work. "Dad, will your guest be staying for lunch?" she said.

Rollie switched off the recorder.

"Miss Kearns, my daughters wish you to have Saturday lunch with us," Rollie said.

Joanna looked at Gloria. "I don't wish to put anybody out," she said.

"Dad always makes too much," Gloria said. "Come on, I'll show you the bathroom if you want to freshen up a bit."

Joanna looked at Rollie. "Arguing with my daughters is a waste of time," he said.

"Alright," Joanna said.

"Tell your sister to heat up the grill," Rollie said.

"Which sister?" Gloria said.

"Pick one," Rollie said.

CHAPTER THREE

While his daughters chatted with Joanna at the picnic table in the backyard, Rollie grilled chicken breasts, thighs and wings. On the side burner, potatoes baked.

Joanna and the girls drank lemonade as they chatted.

Rollie rotated the chicken and potatoes and thought about John Knox. The man was the heavy favorite to win the governorship next year. To the public, he was handsome and respectable, a family man who championed law and order as well as family values.

To the public.

In private, Rollie had no doubt that Knox was like any other professional politician, regardless of party affiliation. Driven by power, and capable of telling any lie to obtain it and hold onto it.

At this stage of his career, Teal wanted nothing to do with John Knox, and Rollie understood that. Teal was ten years from full retirement and a six-figure pension. A dust-up with Knox could result in early retirement and a far less lucrative pension.

Rollie figured his pension was safe, though a man like Knox could certainly lean on the system and get Rollie's private investigator's license pulled.

Rollie rotated the chicken and potatoes one more time.

That license was supposed to fund three college tuitions.

That's how powerful politicians got away with things ordinary people couldn't. Fear. Not the physical kind, but the emotional. Losing a pension, a high paying job, a reputation, a future, all were more frightening than a physical threat.

Rollie stacked chicken and potatoes onto a serving plate and carried it to the table.

"Let's eat," he said.

• • •

After lunch, Rollie and Joanna returned to his office. She signed the retainer document, wrote a check for five thousand, and left her briefcase full of documents.

He asked Grace to call an Uber for Joanna. Then he and Joanna waited in front of the house for the cab to arrive.

"I'll call you at your hotel after I do some research," Rollie said.

Joanna nodded. "I appreciate your taking the time," she said.

Rollie glanced at the large bay window in the living room of the house and spotted his girls peeping out.

"Time, I got," he said. "I will put it to use and get back to you."

The Uber arrived, and Rollie opened the door for Joanna.

"Thank you again," she said.

Rollie watched the cab drive away and then he returned to his office and called Bill Teal.

"You met with Joanna Kearns?" Teal said.

"I did, yes," Rollie said.

"And you sent her on her way?"

"Not quite."

"What's that mean, not quite?" Teal said.

"I put her on retainer," Rollie said.

"Come on, Rollie, you can't possibly believe that bullshit story," Teal said.

"What I believe doesn't matter," Rollie said. "I said I'd give her a couple of days and that's what I'll do."

"To what end?"

"A dead end, most likely," Rollie said.

They hung up, and Rollie played the tape of his conversation with Joanna and made written notes.

．　　　．　　　．

Rollie broke the news to his daughters at the dinner table.

"Grace, you're on baby sitting detail tomorrow morning," Rollie said. "I have to go into the City first thing on business."

"We want to see a movie tomorrow afternoon," Grace said.

"I'll be back before noon," Rollie said.

"Why do we need a baby sitter?" Giselle said.

"Because you and Gloria are minors," Rollie said. "And because I said so. Pass the potatoes."

"How much do I get paid?" Grace said.

"For spending time with your two sisters that you'd be spending time with anyway?" Rollie said.

"One is fun, the other is responsibility," Grace said.

"Alright, Ms. Responsibility, what is your fee for taking care of your own flesh and blood?"

"Jeez, Dad, you make it sound like we're sides of beef hanging in a butcher shop," Giselle said.

"Three movie tickets, popcorn and soda money," Grace said.

"Agreed," Rollie said.

"You should have held out for more," Gloria said.

"And you three do the dishes tonight," Rollie said. "Or I'll really embarrass you by driving you to the movie."

"You wouldn't," Giselle said.

"Try me," Rollie said.

"Let's go, girls, let's get the dishes done," Grace said.

"We have a nice chocolate cake for dessert," Rollie said. "Your mom's recipe."

•   •   •

At his desk, Rollie ate a slice of chocolate cake, drank a mug of coffee, and listened to the taped conversation one more time.

Home at 8:15 on the phone, and at work at 8:45 in time for Tower One to be struck by the hijacked plane.

West End Avenue and 101st Street to Chambers Street in that span of time?

Somebody is lying.

CHAPTER FOUR

Up at six, Rollie made a large stack of Belgian waffles with bacon, ate two waffles and some bacon, and put the rest in the fridge with a note for the girls.

He backed the Buick out of the garage at 7:30 and took Queens Boulevard to the 59th Street Bridge. Sunday Morning traffic was light and he made the bridge in record time, then skirted over to the West Side using the pass at 72nd Street.

Rollie drove north to a parking garage on Broadway and 103rd Street. He walked to West End Avenue and 101st Street and stood in front of the large building where Joanna's sister Julia once lived.

He looked at his watch. The time was 8:35.

Joanna and Julia are on the phone at 8:15 on September 11th, 2001. They chat for a few minutes and then Julia leaves for work.

She has two choices. Walk from 101st to 103rd to catch the local train to 96th Street and then get on the express, or walk directly to 96th Street.

That would be a seven-block walk to the subway station at 103rd, only to wait for a local train to get to 96th Street. No, she would walk directly to 96th street, also a seven-block walk, from West End Avenue.

Rollie checked his watch again. 8:39 when he started walking to the subway at 96th Street. 8:46 when he arrived and that was at a quick pace. Another minute to walk down the stairs, get in line to use her MetroCard.

Onto the platform at, say, 8:48.

It was rush hour. The trains run every two to four minutes. A train arrived at 8:50.

Rollie waited nine minutes for a train to arrive and rode it south to Chambers Street and arrived twenty-three minutes later.

Time spent on the commute was forty one minutes and another five to enter Tower One, then another five to ride up to the 81st floor. Fifty-one minutes total.

There is no way in hell Julia Knox left her apartment at 8:15 and arrived at her office in time for the plane to hit Tower One.

Rollie returned to the subway and was back at his car by 10:45. He stood beside his car for a few minutes and thought.

He pulled out his cell phone and called Joanna Kearns's cell phone. She answered on the third ring.

"Mrs. Kearns, Rollie Finch," Rollie said.

"Good morning," Joanna said.

"Had breakfast yet?" Rollie said.

"Actually, I was just going to brunch at the hotel," Joanna said.

"Wait for me, I'll be there in twenty minutes," Rollie said.

"I'll be in the lobby," Joanna said.

Twenty minutes later, Rollie entered the lobby of the Hilton Hotel on East 42nd Street.

"Brunch is in the main dining hall," Joanna said, meeting him.

Rollie escorted Joanna to the hall and they found a table. A waitress came by and asked for Joanna's room number.

Once they were seated, Rollie said, "Let me tell you why I'm in the City."

Joanna nodded.

"I walked from your sister's old apartment on West End Avenue to the subway and rode it to Chambers Street, and then walked to the site of the old Trade Center. It took me forty-one minutes. On Sunday, when train traffic is light, and I traveled without delays. On a busy Tuesday, with trains backed up, it probably takes longer."

"I told all that to Detective Timmons," Joanna said. "I even showed him the phone bill I got from the phone company. It showed we talked for twelve minutes. From 8:15 to 8:27."

"That bill isn't in the documents you left me," Rollie said.

"I know. I forgot it back home," Joanna said.

"When you get home, can you scan it and email it to me?" Rollie said.

Joanna nodded. "You believe me now, don't you?" she said.

"I was a cop for a long time, Joanna," Rollie said. "What's important isn't what I believe or even know, it's what I can prove."

"But the phone bill proves my sister was home until at least 8:27," Joanna said.

"I've testified in court and worked for enough defense lawyers to know what they would say in court," Rollie said. "You can't prove you spoke to your sister. She might have already left before you called, and you got John Knox on the phone and you chit-chatted with him for twelve minutes."

"But…" Joanna said.

"Can you prove otherwise with one hundred percent certainty?" Rollie said.

"Only my word," Joanna said.

"Against the word of the possible next governor of New York," Rollie said. "Without your sister to corroborate your story."

"I see your point," Joanna said.

"That said, I'd like to earn my retainer," Rollie said.

"You mean, continue on?" Joanna said.

"Yes."

"Thank you."

"You go home tomorrow?"

"Noon flight."

"You have to be at the airport by 10:00," Rollie said. "I'll pick you up at 8:30."

"Mr. Finch, you don't have to…" Joanna said.

"I have to be in the City tomorrow on business, it's no trouble at all," Rollie said. "And we can talk some more on the ride. See you here at 8:30 he said."

.   .   .

Rollie was at his desk around four o'clock when Grace entered the office.

"Dad, the movie starts at 5:00," Grace said.

"It's not rated R, is it?" Rollie said.

"It's a Marvel movie, Dad," Grace said.

"I don't know what that means," Rollie said.

"PG-13."

Rollie gave Grace sixty dollars from his wallet. "What time does it end?"

"7:45," Grace said.

"Are you going to hang out with your friends afterward?" Rollie said.

"For a bit."

"Will you want dinner that late?"

"Probably not."

"Home by 10:00," Rollie said.

"Promise."

After Grace left, Rollie went to the kitchen and made some coffee, then returned to his desk.

He called Bill Teal on the hard line.

"Bill, Rollie," Rollie said.

"If it isn't the gumshoe," Teal said.

"I told you, nobody says gumshoe, Bill," Rollie said. "Be in your office tomorrow?"

"Who wants to know?"

"Me, I do," Rollie said. "Say, around noon?"

"Say I am here around noon, what do you want?" Teal said.

"Fifteen minutes."

"That will cost you lunch and a dozen donuts," Teal said.

"Shouldn't a dozen donuts be considered lunch?" Rollie said.

"Make the dozen mixed," Teal said. "Bye, Rollie."

After hanging up the phone, Rollie changed and hit the step climber in the garage for about an hour, clearing his head, thinking it all through.

How would Julia Knox make it to Tower One in time for the plane to hit?

She should have been on a train, stuck in a tunnel along with tens of thousands of others that day.

Rollie was still in uniform at the time, and he and hundreds of other cops went to the site after the second plane hit and could only watch, helpless to do anything. Then Rollie and lots of other cops stayed there for months, helping to clean up that ugly site.

Nothing of Julia's was ever recovered. However, being on the 81st floor, that wasn't surprising.

Everything would have been incinerated.

Although it was amazing the amount of personal belongings that were recovered in the rubble in the years to come.

After an hour, Rollie took a shower, changed into comfortable sweats, and thought about dinner. He removed a pound of hamburger from the fridge and prepared two burgers, and went to the backyard to start the grill. Then he heated a potato in the microwave.

As he grilled, he went over the problem some more.

Julia Knox.

Did she die in Tower One?

If she didn't die in Tower One, what happened to her?

Why would John Knox want his wife to vanish without a trace?

And how did he fix it so she stayed vanished?

Rollie ate the burgers and baked potato, along with a glass of ginger ale at the backyard picnic table.

Disposing of a human body is a difficult task.

Disposing of a human body, sight unseen, in New York City is a nearly impossible task.

So where is Julia Knox?

Done eating, Rollie gave his brain a rest and went inside and watched an old movie on television for a while. The original *Kiss of Death* from 1947 with Victor Mature. It was quite good. Richard Widmark's portrayal of the crazed killer Tommy Udo was chilling. It ended at 9:45.

Rollie turned the television off and went to the kitchen to wash the few dishes in the sink.

The girls arrived home at exactly ten o'clock.

"Hey, Dad," Grace said.

"You know how to cut things close," Rollie said.

Grace entered the kitchen, while Giselle and Gloria skirted to their bedrooms.

"Good movie," Grace said. "Chris Evans is…"

"Grace, have a seat," Rollie said.

"What?" Grace said.

"At the table, have a seat," Rollie said.

"Can I change first?" Grace said.

"This will only take a minute," Rollie said.

Grace took a chair.

"Gloria, Giselle, the kitchen. Now," Rollie called out.

"In a minute, Dad," Giselle said.

"Now, girls," Rollie said. "It will be worse if I come in there."

Giselle appeared in the doorway of the kitchen with Gloria right behind her.

"Yes, Dad?" Giselle said.

"Have a seat."

"But…" Giselle said.

"Have a seat," Rollie said.

Giselle and Gloria took chairs at the table.

Gloria's face was a mask of panic.

"Yes, Dad," Giselle said.

"Why is Gloria wearing makeup?" Rollie said.

"She's… a girl," Grace said.

"Last time I counted, I had three daughters, yet only one is wearing makeup," Rollie said. "The youngest one."

"It's not her fault, Dad," Grace said. "It's mine."

"Explain," Rollie said.

"We met this boy in her class, a really nice boy," Grace said. "He sat with us at the movie. I put the makeup on Gloria so she wouldn't look so plain."

"Hey!" Gloria said. "How am I plain?"

"Giselle, Gloria, go to your room," Rollie said. "And Gloria, for God's sake, take that paint off your face."

Giselle and Gloria left the kitchen.

Rollie glared at Grace. "What's the rule on dating?"

"No dates until sixteen," Grace said.

"And Gloria is how old?"

"Thirteen," Grace said. "But it wasn't really a date. Giselle and I were there the entire time."

"Then why the need for makeup?" Rollie said. "Your sister is pretty enough as it is, she doesn't need it."

"I'm grounded, aren't I?" Grace said.

"You're the oldest," Rollie said. "When I'm not around it's up to you to be responsible for your sisters. So, I need you to step up and I need to know I can trust you, Grace."

"You can," Grace said.

"One month without the car and one month of doing the dishes alone," Rollie said.

"Yes sir," Grace said.

"Go to bed," Rollie said.

After Grace left the kitchen, Rollie went to his office to make a few more notes. He jotted a couple items on a yellow pad, and looked up when Gloria meekly walked in.

"Yes?" Rollie said.

"Dad, if anybody should be punished, it's me," Gloria said.

"And why is that?"

"I'm the one who wore the makeup."

"Were you the one responsible for the other two?" Rollie said.

"No."

"Goodnight, Gloria," Rollie said.

"Goodnight, Dad," Gloria said.

CHAPTER FIVE

Joanna Kearns was waiting on the sidewalk in front of the Hilton Hotel on East 42nd Street when Rollie arrived at 8:30 the next morning.

Rollie got out to open the door for Joanna, put her luggage in the back, then got behind the wheel and skirted into traffic.

"I feel guilty taking a ride from you," Joanna said.

"Don't. I had to come into the city anyway," Rollie said. "So tell me what you know about John Knox."

"The John Knox I knew back then or what I know today?" Joanna said.

"From the past," Rollie said.

"He was tall and handsome, and my sister fell for him when they met at Columbia," Joanna said. "They got married, but I never had a good feeling about him. Neither did my parents."

"Stop there and tell me why," Rollie said.

"John is one of those men who always say the right thing in public and it always sounds fake, like he rehearsed it," Joanna said. "He had the most perfect hair cuts like a Ken-doll. It just all felt a little off; John's 'performance,' if that's what you want to call it. But my sister loved him and blocked everything else out."

"When did your sister first think about divorcing him?" Rollie said.

"A couple of years before 9/11, she became suspicious he was having affairs," Joanna said. "She confided in me and I told her to confront him."

"Did she?"

"Yes, and he admitted to them and Julia recommended counseling," Joanna said. "To my surprise he agreed, but looking back, it was just a way to keep her quiet."

"You say that because…?" Rollie said.

"Because he didn't stop having affairs," Joanna said. "Two weeks before 9/11, she had lunch with me and said a woman claiming to be from John's office called looking for him. She confronted him and he denied it. He said he didn't need her paranoia on top of everything else."

"And you think she planned to divorce him?" Rollie said.

"And take their daughter with her," Joanna said. "She was just four at the time."

"Do you think he knew her plans?"

"I can't say. We never got to meet for lunch."

"But you suspect it?"

Joanna nodded. "Yes, and I believe it cost my sister her life."

Rollie took the Long Island Expressway East to the airport.

"How long did you talk on the phone that morning?" Rollie said.

"The phone record shows twelve minutes," Joanna said.

"Until about 8:27?" Rollie said.

Joanna nodded.

"What did you talk about?"

"Mostly about meeting for lunch," Joanna said. "She was being very secretive and talked in a whisper. I tried to prod it out of her, but she insisted on telling me at lunch."

As Rollie turned into LaGuardia, he said, "What terminal?"

"Delta."

Rollie drove around the massive airport to the Delta departure terminal. He parked for a moment to get Joanna's suitcase from the back.

"Email me the phone bill when you get home," he said.

"I will," Joanna said.

"I'll call you when I get it," Rollie said.

"Thank you, Rollie," Joanna said. "Maybe nothing will come of this, but I have to try. That monster needs to be stopped."

After Joanna entered the terminal, Rollie drove back to Manhattan, parked near the Midtown Precinct and grabbed a cup of coffee at a donut shop on 41st Street and Broadway.

Twelve minutes.

Could Knox have overheard his wife talking to Joanna that morning and snapped?

Anything, when dealing with the human condition, is possible. Under the right circumstances, a human being is capable of absolutely anything. Rollie had put away some of the most mild-mannered killers, put away family men who murdered their own families.

Knox wouldn't be the first man to fly into a rage and kill his wife, and unfortunately, he wouldn't be the last.

Rollie went to the counter and ordered a dozen fresh donuts and a refill on his coffee. When the donuts were boxed, he left the donut shop and walked two blocks to the Midtown Precinct.

The donuts were still hot when he placed them on Teal's desk.

Teal opened the box and grabbed two donuts. "Good man," he said and took a bite.

"How are you going to eat lunch after two donuts?" Rollie said.

"Watch me," Teal said. "I'll eat the second on the way and drop the box off in the squad room."

As they walked two blocks to a diner, Teal ate the second donut. "My physical is coming up," Teal said. "My wife has me on a diet.

No fat, no butter, no pizza, no salt. Do you know how fucking boring life is without salt, Rollie?"

"I can only imagine," Rollie said.

"I bet you eat all the goddamn salt you want," Teal said.

They reached the diner, went in and grabbed a booth by the window.

"I just…" Rollie said.

"Hold that thought," Teal said as a waitress came to their booth. "I'll have the bacon burger with fries and a Coke."

"A burger with fries and a ginger ale," Rollie said.

After the waitress left, Rollie said, "I just left Joanna Kearns. She has some damaging evidence that needs to be looked at."

"So, look at it," Teal said.

"Bill, would you just listen," Rollie said.

"No, you listen, Rollie," Teal said. "There isn't a captain in New York that would allow an investigation into golden boy Knox. Once he's governor, a lot of blue heads will roll if they tried."

"I didn't ask you to," Rollie said. "I asked you to listen."

Teal sighed.

"Julia Knox was on the phone with her sister from 8:15 until 8:27 the morning of 9/11," Rollie said. "How did she go from 101st Street and West End Avenue to Tower One in eighteen minutes?"

Teal looked at Rollie.

"I timed it door-to-door on Sunday," Rollie said. "It took me 41 minutes and that's without rush hour traffic and the usual delays."

"Maybe she had the time wrong?" Teal said.

"She has the phone bill," Rollie said.

The waitress arrived with lunch. Teal added salt to his and bit into the burger. "I should have known better than to send her to you," he said. "As anal as you are, Rollie."

"If she left her apartment exactly at 8:27, she would have arrived at around 9:11, a good half hour after the first plane hit Tower One. So, how did she die on the 81st floor that day?"

Teal sighed. "What do you want from me, Rollie? A million things could have happened—she could have hung around on the street while the whole thing collapsed on her; some jumper could have landed on her."

"I want Knox's financial and criminal records," Rollie said.

"Have you lost your mind?" Teal said.

"A long time ago, but I still want them," Rollie said.

"And will you pay my pension with benefits when I get kicked off the job?" Teal said.

"I'm not going to advertise in the *Times* where I got it from, for God's sake," Rollie said. "And it was you who brought her to me, Bill."

Teal looked at Rollie and sighed.

"If I do this, it's between us and no one else," Teal said.

"For Christ sake, Bill," Rollie said.

"Give me forty-eight hours," Teal said. "But Rollie, anything you uncover comes straight to me."

"I thought you said…"

"Never mind what I said."

"Anything I find is yours, Bill," Rollie said.

Teal looked at Rollie's plate. "You gonna eat those fries?"

After lunch, walking back to the precinct, Teal said, "I'm not saying you're on to something, Rollie, but the time thing is a puzzle."

"Puzzles are meant to be solved," Rollie said.

"Not all of them. Thanks for lunch."

CHAPTER SIX

Rollie carried two shopping bags of food into the kitchen and put everything away, and then found the girls playing a video game in the living room.

"What game is that?" Rollie said.

"The Farm," Giselle said.

"What do you do?" Rollie said.

"Make a farm," Grace said.

"I see," Rollie said. "I'll be in the office."

"Hey, those are my pigs," he heard Gloria say as he left the room.

Rollie went for a glass of ginger ale and took it to his office. He scribbled a few notes in his notebook and then did a computer search on John Knox.

The information was extensive, mostly because of his bid to become the next governor.

In 2001, Knox was a junior partner in a mid-level Manhattan law firm, making eighty-five thousand a year. Great pay for Queens or Brooklyn, but hardly a fortune for Manhattan.

He was thirty-two at the time.

After 9/11, Knox apparently fell apart. He quit his position at the law firm, supposedly to stay home and care for his four-year-old daughter. He lived on his savings and insurance money from Julia's policy at work.

Knox attended grief counseling arranged by the city. He must have had a great deal of input into the article because it stressed how difficult the first year was for him and his daughter.

Living on his savings and his wife's insurance money, Knox fell into despair until he started attending grief counseling meetings for the loved ones of 9/11 victims. It was there he met his second wife, Dana. She had lost her husband, and had a young son. They struck up a friendship. After a year, it turned into a budding romance.

They married in late 2003.

In early 2004, Knox went to work for a large law firm in Midtown and after several years, became a partner. He moved the family to a posh condo building on the East Side.

In 2010, Knox was elected to the Manhattan Town Council. Knox's star continued to rise. In 2012, he was selected to run as lieutenant governor, a position he's held for the past seven years.

Last year he declared his candidacy for governor, and was currently the heavy favorite to win the election. Knox, as was the present governor, was a registered independent.

His platform was law and order, jobs and education, and the economy.

In other words, same bullshit, different package with a better haircut.

Rollie searched for recent photos of the happy couple. He found many. Now fifty-one, Knox was tall, well-built and had perfect hair and a dazzling smile. Dana Knox, now forty-nine, was a beautiful brunette who, thanks to makeup, botox, and the right photographer, could pass for thirty-five.

Knox's daughter, now in her early twenties, was a good-looking woman who resembled her mother. Dana's son, also in his early twenties, had his mother's hair and eyes.

A side note was that in 2006, Knox legally adopted Dana's son.

The entire article was pure puff.

Rollie found another article online from six months ago, a five-page spread in *People* magazine.

The *Sunday Times* did a large piece on Knox in their Metropolitan Section in which they nearly anointed him the next governor.

It was noted that Knox recently opened a campaign headquarters on 51st and Broadway.

Rollie had enough of John Knox for one night and went to the kitchen to start dinner.

He marinated three pounds of boneless chicken thighs in Italian dressing for fifteen minutes. Then he rinsed six potatoes and brought them to the backyard grill and got them started.

Back in the kitchen, Rollie put a pound of asparagus in the steamer.

The girls were still in the living room. "Girls, set the table," he said. "And bring the chicken out in ten minutes."

Rollie returned to the backyard and rotated the potatoes.

John Knox, what wasn't in those puff pieces? What demons live in your head that come out to play after dark?

Women?

Drugs?

Gambling?

Gloria came out with the platter of chicken.

"Table set?" Rollie said.

"Grace is doing it," Gloria said.

She set the platter on the wing of the grill, and Rollie used a large fork to place the chicken thighs on the hot surface.

"Dad, is Grace still punished?" Gloria said.

"Yes," Rollie said.

"Well, Giselle and I talked it over and we think we should be punished, too," Gloria said.

"You do?" Rollie said.

"Grace put the makeup on me, but all three of us agreed to do it, so we're all guilty and we all should be punished," Gloria said.

"When school starts up again, who is in charge of the classroom?" Rollie said.

"My teacher."

"And if every kid in that class fails, who is to blame?"

"Is this a trick question?"

"Nope."

"We fail, but it's the teacher's responsibility," Gloria said.

"You and Giselle may have gone along with it, but it was Grace's responsibility and she knows that," Rollie said.

Gloria nodded.

"Tell your sisters ten minutes," Rollie said.

Ten minutes later, Rollie carried the chicken and baked potatoes inside to the table.

Grace seemed perfectly normal during the meal and afterward. She washed, dried, and put away the dirty dishes without so much as a hint of resentment.

He took a mug of coffee to the office and checked emails.

Joanna Kearns had sent an email with a copy of the phone bill as an attachment. Rollie opened the attachment and printed it.

The first call on September 11, 2001, was to Julia Knox's number. The call lasted from 8:15 until 8:27. The next call was at 11:31 and lasted just four minutes.

Joanna had said she tried calling a dozen or more times and John Knox didn't answer until 11:31.

Rollie printed out a second copy for Teal.

Then he called Joanna's cell phone. She answered on the second ring. "I sent you the phone bill," she said.

"I just printed it," Rollie said. "And I see the second call you made at 11:31 lasted just four minutes."

"John was out of it," Joanna said. "He had taken medicine for the flu and had been sleeping, so he said. Then he got all hysterical and hung up. My parents also called and he hung up on them, too."

"Okay, thanks. I'll call you tomorrow," Rollie said.

"Goodnight," Joanna said.

After hanging up, Rollie sat at his desk for a long time and thought.

When he finally closed up the office, the girls were already in bed. He took a can of ginger ale to the backyard and sat at the patio table.

From 8:27 until 11:31, what were you doing, John Knox?

And why?

CHAPTER SEVEN

Rollie removed Georgia's notebook of recipes from a drawer at the kitchen counter and found the one for buttermilk pancakes. All her recipes were handwritten in black ink. She had a rating system and made a red star next to the ones that she preferred.

The buttermilk recipe had two red stars next to it. As Rollie prepared the batter in a large mixing bowl, he put some bacon in a pan to cook.

While he waited for the batter to set, he sipped coffee and stirred the bacon.

Grace entered the kitchen first. "Morning, Dad," she said.

"Good morning, honey," Rollie said.

Grace opened a cabinet and set the table. Giselle and Gloria entered the kitchen and immediately pitched in.

"Mom's recipe book," Grace said.

"Yes it is," Rollie said.

"Can I make them?" Grace said.

"Why not?" Rollie said.

Grace read through the instructions, heated a large skillet and melted some butter in it. Then she used a scoop to place four round pancakes in the skillet.

Giselle took charge of the bacon, and Gloria filled four glasses with orange juice.

"Call me when it's ready," Rollie said.

Rollie went to his office to check emails. Then he called Bill Teal.

"I need until the end of the day, Rollie," Teal said.

"Fine. Bring it to my house. Stay for dinner," Rollie said.

"My wife will…"

"Serve you lettuce and carrots like a bunny in a cage," Rollie said. "At my house, you'll get real food with lots of fat and salt and flavor."

"You're an evil man, Rollie, you know that?" Teal said.

"6:30. Don't be late," Rollie said.

Gloria entered the office. "Breakfast," she said.

At the table, Rollie sampled the pancakes. "As good as your mother used to make," he said.

"Thanks, Dad," Grace said. "We took turns."

"Good, then you can take turns again," Rollie said. "Your uncle Bill is coming to dinner tonight, and I'd like you three to make the meal."

"What should we make?" Grace said.

"You pick. Go through your mom's book and pick what you want," Rollie said. "Then we'll take a trip to the store."

After breakfast, Grace brought the dirty dishes to the sink. As she washed, Giselle dried and Gloria stacked. Rollie watched for a moment. They were sisters through and through.

Rollie took a mug of coffee back to his office.

He read the articles on Knox again and then searched for additional information. Almost across the board, Knox was portrayed as a candidate for sainthood.

Even saints were sinners at some point.

Rollie took a chance Joanna was home and called her cell number.

"Rollie, good morning," Joanna said.

"Do you have a few minutes?" Rollie said.

"Of course."

"I've been reading puff-piece after puff-piece on Knox since yesterday," Rollie said. "Nobody is as perfect as they make this guy out to be. Can you tell me any secrets about him your sister might have confided in you?"

"Besides his affairs?" Joanna said.

"Yes."

"He was a mean drunk," Joanna said. "Julia said he never hit her, but he could get quite nasty. And he liked to gamble in Atlantic City."

"One article said he fell into despair after your sister's death," Rollie said. "Was he drinking heavily?"

"From what little I saw of him, he was," Joanna said. "He wouldn't let me see my niece."

"Are your parents still alive?" Rollie said.

"My mother is," Joanna said.

"I'd like to talk to her at some point," Rollie said.

"She's retired and living in Florida," Joanna said. "In fact, I'll be visiting her in a few weeks while school is still out."

"Can you think of anything else?" Rollie said.

"Not at the moment," Joanna said.

"If you think of anything, call me right away," Rollie said.

"I will," Joanna said. "Rollie, he did it, didn't he?"

"He may well have, but the game has just started," Rollie said.

"I know. I'll call you if I remember anything else that might be useful."

After hanging up, Rollie searched for additional articles on Knox and found several and read every word.

It was almost as if every reporter was afraid to criticize Knox for any reason. Were they under marching orders from their editors? Did they really believe in Knox to such a high degree that they willingly lathered him in praise?

Kennedy.

They were hoping for another JFK.

If he wasn't born royalty, they would manufacture him into royalty. From governor to president in one fell swoop.

Rollie went to the kitchen where the girls were reading from Georgia's cookbook.

"Lasagna," Grace said. "We want to make lasagna."

"But we don't have the ingredients in the house," Gloria said.

"Well, let's go get them," Rollie said. "Make a list and we'll head to the store."

Rollie drove the girls to the large grocery store about a mile from the house where he let them do the shopping.

At the front of the store were benches and Rollie took a seat.

After reading all of the coverage on Knox, it was obvious he was being groomed for a run at the White House. He'd be, what, fifty-five by that time, the perfect age to run for president.

"Dad, what does Uncle Bill like for dessert?" Gloria said as she approached the bench.

"When we were partners and went to lunch, he'd always get warm apple pie with a scoop of ice cream," Rollie said.

Gloria nodded and dashed away.

Once the girls were in a checkout line, Rollie met them there to pay for the groceries.

Back at home, the girls carefully planned the lasagna dinner and Rollie went to his office.

He sat at his desk and thought about murder. How did Knox kill his wife? Dose her with something? Was he the kind of guy that could break her with a hammer, would he grip his hands around her throat?

There are many ways of killing a person that don't involve a gun or a knife.

A gun makes noise, a lot of noise. Neighbors would have heard the gunshot. A knife is silent, but as with a gun, leaves a blood trail behind that is nearly impossible to clean up.

Blood is visible under UV light for decades.

Knox was a big man and easily capable of strangling his wife if enraged.

Was he enraged?

Did he overhear the conversation between Julia and Joanna, confront Julia, and fly into a rage and kill her?

Say he did, what did he do with the body?

The body of an adult woman isn't so easily disposed of, especially when you live in an apartment.

Did he dismember her with a knife?

Much easier said than done, despite what you see in gangster movies. Even a skilled butcher would have a difficult time cutting up a human being without leaving a trace behind. Rollie had seen and heard of the so-called mis-memberers, where the killer starts down the road of dismembering his victim but realizes the effort involved and stops halfway through sawing an arm or hacking a leg.

So, what did he do with Julia Knox?

Rollie picked up the phone and called Joanna. She answered on the second ring again.

"I was just thinking about you," Joanna said. "I remembered something. I don't know if it's important, but it's something Julia confided in me."

"At this stage, everything is important," Rollie said.

"Well, early on in their marriage, Julia told me that John wanted to play the choke game during sex, but she refused," Joanna said. "She said he never brought it up again."

"That's good, thank you," Rollie said. "The reason I called: how big a woman was your sister?"

"At that time, she was five-foot-three and weighed, I don't know, one-ten, a hundred and fifteen pounds," Joanna said.

"So, she was tiny?"

"Very."

"Thank you, Joanna, I'll call you again soon," Rollie said.

After hanging up, Rollie went to his bedroom to change into sweats. The girls were in the kitchen, pouring over the cookbook as if it was a science project. He returned to the garage and did an hour on the step climber.

The choke game during sex. You choke your partner during sex to heighten their orgasm.

Knox liked to use his hands.

How difficult would it be for a six-foot-four-inch man to overpower a five-foot-two-inch woman?

Not very.

So, what did he do with the body?

• • •

At 6:30, Rollie opened the door to Bill Teal. The girls greeted him with warm hugs and kisses.

"Dinner in fifteen minutes," Grace said.

"We'll be right there," Rollie said.

Teal and Rollie went to the garage where Teal removed a thick envelope from his jacket pocket.

"Financial and police reports," Teal said.

Rollie gave Teal a copy of the phone bill. Teal looked at it, nodded and said, "Son of a bitch."

"We'll talk later," Rollie said. "The girls have been working on dinner all afternoon."

"What's on the menu?" Teal said.

"Homemade lasagna, Georgia's recipe."

"Sausage layered in?"

"Of course."

"Why are we in the garage?"

•　　•　　•

"That was a fine dinner, girls. Really excellent," Teal said.

"We made dessert," Grace said.

"Warm apple pie with vanilla ice cream," Giselle.

"We know you and Dad want to talk business, so we'll bring it to you," Grace said.

"Thanks, girls," Teal said.

Rollie and Teal went to the office.

"More like their mother every day," Teal said.

"Yeah."

"So, what do you got that's new?"

"You saw the time on the bill," Rollie said. "Even if she grew wings, she couldn't make it in eighteen minutes."

"No, she couldn't," Teal admitted.

"Knox had a thing about choking his wife during sex," Rollie said.

Teal looked at Rollie.

"Joanna told me Julia Knox confided in her," Rollie said. "Julia Knox was tiny; John Knox is John Wayne size. He could have choked her to death in a matter of minutes."

"And done what with the body?" Teal said. "Even a tiny body isn't easy to dispose of, especially in an apartment."

"He found a way," Rollie said. "I'm sure of it."

"How?"

"I don't know how yet."

"Well, when you do know how, don't keep it to yourself."

"Wouldn't dream of it," Rollie said.

"Anything else?"

"Back then, besides countless affairs, Knox was drinking and gambling quite a bit," Rollie said. "None of which made the puff pieces the media has written about him."

Grace, Giselle, and Gloria entered the office with two plates of apple pie and ice cream and more coffee.

"Oh, thank you girls," Teal said.

"Welcome, Uncle Bill," Grace said.

After the girls left the office, Rollie said, "Where is Timmons?"

"How the hell do I know?" Teal said. "He retired eight years ago."

"Can you find him for me?" Rollie said.

"What's he going to tell you that isn't in his report?" Teal said.

"All you have to do is find out where they send his pension check," Rollie said. "I'll do the rest."

Teal sighed.

"Thanks, Bill," Rollie said.

"Just remember what I said about sharing," Teal said.

"*Mi casa, su casa*," Rollie said.

"Call me tomorrow after you read all this crap I left you," Teal said.

"I'll walk you out," Rollie said.

They went to the kitchen where the girls were on clean-up detail, and after hugs for Teal, Rollie walked him out to his car.

Before he got in, Teal said, "I hope you know what you're doing."

"Makes two of us," Rollie said.

After Teal drove away, Rollie returned to the kitchen. "Girls, I thought Grace's punishment was that she had to do the dishes for one month alone," he said.

"We found a technical flaw in your punishment," Giselle said.

47

"This should be good," Rollie said.

"You said Grace had to wash the dishes," Giselle said. "And she is."

"But I'm drying and Giselle is putting them away, so…" Gloria said.

"Technically, we're within the guidelines of your punishment," Giselle said.

"And besides, we're sisters," Gloria said.

They waited for Rollie to pop his top, but he nodded and said, "Carry on, then."

As Rollie turned to enter his office, Grace said, "Dad?"

"Yes?"

"What should we make for breakfast?" Grace said.

Rollie smiled and said, "Surprise me."

CHAPTER EIGHT

Rollie sat at his desk and read the documents Teal gave him.

After 9/11, Knox quit his position at the law firm. There was forty thousand in a joint savings account that he lived on until Julia's insurance policy kicked in, from which he received a one-hundred-thousand-dollar settlement. Julia also had forty-seven-thousand in a 401K account that went to him as well.

Close to two hundred thousand, all told.

His apartment was rent controlled, but still cost fifteen hundred a month. Eighteen thousand a year in rent, plus utilities, food and medical expenses for him and his daughter.

There should have been adequate money to last for a few years, but there wasn't.

In 2002, Knox applied for legal aid to help support his daughter.

That was about the time he started attending grief counseling and soon after that, he received a four-hundred-thousand-dollar settlement from the city for the loss of his wife. He ended the legal aid shortly thereafter.

In 2003, Knox married his second wife and he returned to work at a larger law firm as a junior partner at an annual salary of one hundred and twenty-five thousand in 2004.

When he made full partner in 2006, his salary was four-hundred-thousand a year plus bonuses. The real money was in the bonuses.

By 2010, the year Knox became a city councilman, he was a millionaire several times over, and he moved the family to a posh, East Side residence.

After that came the lieutenant governorship of New York, the second in command of the state.

The position paid one-hundred and fifty thousand a year, chump change compared to what he was used to earning.

It wasn't the money.

It was the power.

Rollie predicted that if he won, Knox would serve one term as governor before running for president.

His police record was next to nonexistent. Except for the report filed by Timmons, there wasn't much at all. A parking ticket in 1997 for missing alternate side of the street parking, and a speeding ticket a week after 9/11 on the New York Thruway South at 1:34 in the morning. He was doing 77 in a 55.

Odd, that was just one week after his wife supposedly died in Tower One.

Where did you go, John?

What were you doing?

Why the hurry to get back?

The ashes at the Trade Center were still hot, and your wife dead less than a week, and you're driving around on the New York Thruway.

Why?

It struck Rollie that Knox wasn't a spur-of-the-moment kind of guy. Everything he does is carefully planned out in advance, so would he take a midnight ride for no reason one week after losing his wife?

When Georgia died, Rollie barely spoke for a month. The girls were younger and just as devastated as he, and they huddled together for support until they were able to rejoin the world.

The last thing he did was take long drives on the thruway in the middle of the night.

Because he didn't have a reason to.

Knox had a reason.

Rollie decided he wasn't going to find that reason tonight and called it a night.

The girls were watching a movie on television and he joined them for a bit. It was some sappy romantic comedy that had the girls weeping at the ending.

"Why did they have to kill the dog?" Gloria wept and went to her room.

"Bummer," Giselle said and went to her room.

"TV's yours, Dad," Grace said and went to her room.

Rollie sighed. "Well, *I* didn't kill the dog," he said, and turned the TV off and went to his room.

CHAPTER NINE

After breakfast, Rollie was reading all of his notes and reports again when Teal called.

"Al Timmons retired to the Florida Keys," Teal said. "Got a small condo on the water on Islamorada Key. Want the address?"

"Yes."

Rollie wrote the address on his legal pad. "Thanks, Bill."

"What are you going to do now?" Teal said.

"Go see Al Timmons," Rollie said.

"*Mi casa, su casa*, remember, Rollie," Teal said.

"You'll be the first I call," Rollie said.

"Yeah, who's the second?"

After hanging up with Teal, Rollie thought for a few minutes and then called Joanna.

She sounded happy to hear from him.

"Joanna, I was wondering when you're going to see your mother."

"I was planning on going in a couple of weeks," Joanna said.

"Would it be alright if I spoke to your mother in person?" Rollie said.

"In person?"

"Yes. I have to go to Florida next week on another matter, and I thought I could talk to her while I'm there," Rollie said.

"I suppose I could set up a time with her then," Joanna said.

"Where does she live?"

"About thirty miles north of Orlando."

"Can you set it up for Tuesday?" Rollie said.

"I'll call her and arrange it," Joanna said.

"Perfect. Thanks, Joanna," Rollie said.

"I'll call you back later today," Joanna said.

Rollie went to the kitchen where the girls were reading Georgia's cookbook.

"Get dressed," Rollie said.

The girls all froze up.

"Ten minutes, let's go," Rollie said.

•   •   •

Rollie parked in the small lot reserved for the Forest Hills Travel Agency on Queens Boulevard.

"Are we going somewhere?" Grace said.

"Where are we going?" Giselle said.

"Is it someplace fun?" Gloria said.

"We're not going anywhere unless you quit asking questions so we can go in first," Rollie said.

Once inside, Rollie and the girls met with the travel agent.

"I'd like three days in Orlando and three days in the Florida Keys on Islamorada," Rollie said.

Grace, Giselle, and Gloria gasped in unison.

"Let's talk about this," the travel agent said.

•   •   •

"Three days in Orlando and three days in the Keys," Grace said.

"How come, Dad?" Giselle said.

"I need to go to Florida on business for a few days," Rollie said. "I thought I'd take you along, provided Grace is up to the task of being the adult."

"You mean baby-sitter?" Gloria said.

"Would you rather I hire a nanny for a week and went to Florida alone?" Rollie said.

"I'll be the adult in the room," Grace said.

"Good." Rollie said. "Then we'll all have a nice vacation before school starts up again."

"Oh my God," Grace said.

"What?" Rollie said.

"We need new clothes!" Grace said.

"You just bought a whole new wardrobe," Rollie said.

"Those are *school* clothes, Dad," Grace said.

"We need Florida clothes," Giselle said.

"We don't want to look like geeks, Dad," Gloria said.

"Fine," Rollie said. "We'll go to the mall tomorrow."

Once they reached home, the girls poured over the brochures in the kitchen while Rollie went to his office.

He read the report filed by Timmons on September 4, 2001. After speaking with Joanna Kearns, Timmons went to see John Knox at his apartment. Knox appeared disheveled and exhausted, which was probably normal under the circumstances. Timmons did a search of the apartment and found nothing unusual.

Joanna Kearns pleaded with Timmons to investigate the phone call, and Timmons took it to Judge Henry Laudemire, who rejected it on insufficient evidence for a warrant.

On September 18th, Timmons closed the file on John Knox.

Rollie couldn't fault Timmons, not really. The city had been knocked on its ass, and the entire country was reeling from the blow. Under the circumstances, there was very little Timmons could have done. And anybody higher up than him was now interested only in terrorism, not your run-of-the-mill domestic murder.

Rollie went to the kitchen where the girls were making lists on a pad.

"Our activities list," Grace explained.

"Carry on," Rollie said and went to his room to change into sweats. He did an hour on the step climber and thought about what he would have done had he drawn the case twenty years ago.

Maybe the same as Timmons, but when things quieted down again, he would have gone back for another look at Knox.

It may have been a waste of time or it may have been fruitful, but he wouldn't have closed the case so soon.

After one hour, Rollie went to take a shower. He tossed on clean sweatpants and a tee-shirt and met the girls in the kitchen. They were going through the recipe book.

"We're trying to decide between baked chicken or breaded pork chops," Grace said.

"Do we have either?" Rollie said.

"We have pork chops, a dozen of them," Grace said.

"Then, guess what we're having for dinner," Rollie said. "Want some help?"

"We got it, Dad," Grace said.

"Ring the dinner bell when it's ready," Rollie said.

He went to his office and sat at his desk. A moment later, Joanna called on her cell phone.

"I spoke to my mother and she is very anxious to talk to you," Joanna said.

"Then, I shall see you both on Tuesday," Rollie said. "I'll call you on Monday for directions."

"If I think of anything, I'll call you right away," Joanna said.

"Same here," Rollie said.

After hanging up, Rollie returned to the kitchen.

"Mom's recipe calls for twenty-five minutes, so, dinner in fifteen," Grace said.

"How is your activates list coming?" Rollie said.

"Almost done," Gloria said.

"The rice is boiling over," Rollie said.

"I got it," Gloria said.

Fifteen minutes later, they sat down to dinner.

"So, what's on your activities list?" Rollie said.

"Disney World and Universal in Orlando, and if there's time, Sea World," Grace said.

"In Islamorada, we'd like to go to Theater of the Sea and see the dolphin show," Gloria said.

"Sounds good," Rollie said.

"We haven't gone anywhere together since Mom…" Grace said.

Gloria looked at Grace, who suddenly seemed on the verge of tears.

"I'm sorry, honey," Grace said.

"We all miss your mother," Rollie said. "But she would want us to carry on and enjoy life as a family."

Gloria nodded.

"Let's eat," Grace said. "Mom would want us to eat."

CHAPTER TEN

After shopping all morning at the mall in Valley Stream, Rollie treated the girls to lunch at the food court.

"Why can't I have a bikini?" Gloria said.

"Because you're thirteen," Rollie said.

"We forgot sun block," Grace said.

"We can get that anywhere," Rollie said.

"What about sun hats?" Grace said. "We need some cool looking sun hats."

"They had some nice ones at the Bikini Hut," Gloria said.

"Nice try," Rollie said. "Hats only."

•　　•　　•

Rollie went to his office while the girls tried on everything they had just tried on at the mall, something their mother always did and he never understood.

He called Teal at his office.

"I'm headed down to Florida next week to see Al Timmons," Rollie said.

"Tell him I said hi," Teal said.

"I'll also be talking to Julia Knox's mother," Rollie said. "She lives in Orlando."

"Talking to her because…?" Teal said.

"Because Timmons didn't," Rollie said.

"I'm glad you're not fact-checking any of *my* old cases," Teal said.

"How about lunch tomorrow?" Rollie said.

"You buying?"

"It was my idea."

"One o'clock."

"And bring…"

"Donuts for the squad, I know," Rollie said.

After hanging up with Teal, Rollie changed into sweats and did an hour on the step climber.

He gathered his thoughts and worked out a plan for tomorrow, and when the hour had passed, he grabbed a shower and changed into slacks and a Polo shirt.

The girls were in the living room, playing a video game on the television. A knight with a gleaming sword was slaying a giant dragon.

Rollie suggested that they go out to dinner, and asked the girls to pick a place.

Rollie went to his desk and put his thoughts for tomorrow on paper.

Grace entered the office and said, "We decided on The Roma. I called and made a reservation for 6:00. Okay?"

Rollie glanced at the clock on his desk. "Be ready to leave at a quarter of."

Grace nodded and left the office.

Rollie checked his emails and replied to two law firms that regularly used his services for investigative work. He set up appointments for later in the week.

At 5:45, he met the girls at the car and drove to The Roma in Forest Hills.

The food was Italian and quite good. Table talk was of the pending trip to Florida and the things they were going to do on their vacation.

"Dad, you haven't said anything about what you want to do," Grace said.

"I have an idea, but it's a surprise," Rollie said.

"What about dessert?" Gloria said. "Should we get dessert?"

"I have an idea about that, too," Rollie said.

After dinner, Rollie drove them to The Dugout, an ice cream stand designed to resemble the dugout of the New York Yankees. They got scoops of ice cream served in mini plastic baseball hats.

"This was Mom's favorite place," Grace said.

"It still is," Rollie said.

"So, what's your secret idea?" Giselle said.

"If I told you, it wouldn't be a secret," Rollie said.

"Do we get to keep the little hats?" Gloria said.

"If you want," Rollie said.

When they returned home, the girls watched a movie while Rollie went to his office.

He checked his notes. He needed to be at 101st Street and West End Avenue by nine o'clock so he would have time to meet Teal for lunch. Then he planned to go to the Knox campaign headquarters office on Broadway.

When he returned to the living room, all three girls were in tears.

"Why do they always kill off the dog?" Gloria said and ran to her room.

Rollie sighed. "Tomorrow, I have to leave early to head into the city," he said. "Grace, you're in charge. I expect…"

"Responsibility."

CHAPTER ELEVEN

Rollie parked in a garage on Broadway and 103rd Street and walked to the building on West End Avenue.

Traffic was brutal and he didn't arrive until 9:30.

A man of about fifty was bringing garbage cans from the sidewalk through an alleyway to the basement.

"Excuse me," Rollie said, his wallet at the ready. "My name is Rollie Finch and I'm a private investigator."

"No kidding," the man said with a heavy Spanish accent.

Rollie held up his identification.

"Like in the movies," the man said. "What can I do for you?"

"Have you worked for the building long?" Rollie said.

"Twenty-seven years. Why?"

"I've been hired to do a background check on John Knox," Rollie said. "Do you remember him at all?"

"His wife died on 9/11," the man said. "Now he's running for governor."

"If you have a few minutes, what can you tell me about him from back then?" Rollie said.

"Not much," the man said. "I hardly saw him except in the hallways. I'd be mopping and he'd pass me right by, never saying hello. He was one of those guys, if you weren't wearing a designer suit, you were invisible."

"What about his wife Julia?"

"Now, there was a nice lady. Always had a smile and a good morning. It's a shame what happened to her."

"Are there many people in the building from that time who might remember them?" Rollie said.

"Mrs. Birmbaum. Give me a few minutes to finish up here and I'll take you up to see her."

"Thanks. What's your name?" Rollie said.

"Hector."

Rollie waited on the front stairs until Hector was finished, and then Hector took Rollie to the fifth floor, to apartment 5E.

"She's a bit hard of hearing," Hector said as he rang the bell. "Mrs. Birmbaum, it's Hector."

The door opened and a woman in her seventies looked at Hector. "Is something wrong?" she said.

"No, dear," Hector said. "This is Mr. Finch. He's a private detective doing background research on John Knox."

"Well, come in. I'll put on some tea," Mrs. Birmbaum said. "You too, Hector."

Five minutes later, Rollie, Hector, and Mrs. Birmbaum sat down to tea at the kitchen table.

"So Mr. Finch, what kind of information are you looking for?" Mrs. Birmbaum said.

"Background material mostly," Rollie said. "Have you heard of the October surprise?"

"Every election they spring something nasty in October," Mrs. Birmbaum said.

"That's right," Rollie said. "So, it's best to get it out front now, well before the election. Dirt isn't a surprise if everybody already knows."

"I'm afraid I can tell you very little about Mr. Knox," Mrs.

Birmbaum said. "He's what I call a cold fish. He acted like it would kill him to say hello to a person. Hector, how is your tea?"

"Fine, Mrs. Birmbaum," Hector said.

"Now his wife Julia, there was a friendly, outgoing woman. A real peach," Mrs. Birmbaum said. "Always had a smile, always said hello, and sometimes we'd have tea together. It's a crime what happened to her."

"Did you ever hear them argue?" Rollie said.

"Through these walls?" Mrs. Birmbaum said. "This building is over one hundred years old and the walls are over a foot thick. You could fire a shotgun next door and I wouldn't hear it."

"What about after Julia died?" Rollie said. "There are stories about Knox's drinking and depression."

"It's true he was a mess, but it was to be expected the way she was taken from him," Mrs. Birmbaum said. "Sometimes I'd see him in the hallway, unshaven and dirty. He didn't work for several years. But he got counseling, got a new job, and bounced back the way we're supposed to after a great loss. He was still a cold fish, though."

"How about their daughter, did you much about know her?" Rollie said.

"Oh, several times I would babysit her when they had a function to go to, things like that," Mrs. Birmbaum said. "She was a wonderful child."

"When was the last time you baby-sat her, can you remember?" Rollie said.

"Odd that you mention that," Mrs. Birmbaum said. "A week or so after his wife died, he knocked on my door. He said he was going crazy sitting around the house and wanted to go for a drive in the country, and asked if I could watch the baby. Naturally I felt terrible for him, so I said yes. I had just retired after thirty years of teaching and I had the time."

"How long was he gone?" Rollie said.

"Just overnight."

"Did he say where he went?"

"No, and I didn't want to pry into his suffering."

"And that was the last time you sat for the child?" Rollie said.

"Yes. After that, he hardly spoke to me at all. Like I said, a cold fish," Mrs. Birmbaum said. "When he moved out, he didn't even say goodbye."

"Thank you for your time and the tea," Rollie said.

Hector rode down with Rollie in the elevator. "This ain't no background check, is it?" Hector said.

"Hector, how do the tenants dispose of their trash?" Rollie said.

"They bring it to the service elevator and put it in the bin," Hector said. "In the morning, I collect it and put it in the cans."

"Where is the service elevator?" Rollie said.

"At the end of every hall on every floor."

On the first floor, Rollie and Hector walked to the service elevator. "Is it ever locked?" Rollie said.

"No," Hector said. "You need a key to enter the lobby, so the tenants want the service elevator open all night for trash."

"And it goes to the basement?"

Hector nodded. "I'll show you."

Rollie and Hector rode down to the basement on the service elevator. The basement was large, with several work benches, a storage area, and a room with the garbage cans in it.

There was one door to the street.

"Locked?" Rollie said.

"From the outside," Hector said. "Fire laws say it must be able to be unlocked from the inside."

"Where is your apartment?" Rollie said.

"First floor, 1A," Hector said.

"Can we go out this way?" Rollie said.

Hector opened the door, and he and Rollie walked to the courtyard, through the alleyway to the street.

Rollie fished out his card and a fifty dollar bill and gave both to Hector. "If you think of anything, give me a call," Rollie said.

"This ain't about no background check, is it?" Hector asked again.

•   •   •

Rollie set a box of a dozen donuts on Teal's desk. "Ready for lunch?" he said.

Teal opened the box, removed two donuts and set them on a napkin. "We'll drop the rest off to the detectives on the way out.

Rollie and Teal walked a few blocks to the diner. Teal ordered a bowl of chili, a bacon cheese burger with fries, and a Coke. Rollie went with a chicken sandwich and ginger ale.

"So, why the free lunch?" Teal said.

"Knox's speeding ticket," Rollie said.

"What about it?" Teal said.

"One week after 9/11, he has his neighbor watch his daughter, and takes an overnight drive to the country," Rollie said. "Why?"

"Maybe he felt a drive to the country would calm his nerves?" Teal said.

"So much so that he needed a baby-sitter?"

"Your point is?"

"I checked that building, Bill. A tenant told me the walls are a foot thick and you couldn't here a thing in the next apartment," Rollie said. "They have an old service elevator used for garbage. It goes down to the basement and right to the street. You could carry a body out that way at night, sight unseen. He loads her into his car and takes off for parts unknown and gets a ticket on the way back."

Teal looked at Rollie.

"He could have done it, Bill," Rollie said.

"Any proof of any of this?"

"None whatsoever," Rollie said.

Teal sighed. "See anything in his finances?"

"Nothing a judge would give you a search warrant for," Rollie said.

"The guy is going to be our next governor, you bet your ass no judge will issue a search warrant," Teal said.

"He could have done it, Bill," Rollie said.

"Bring me something that said he *did* do it, and I'll go with it," Teal said.

"I will," Rollie said.

"That's what I'm afraid of," Teal said.

•   •   •

Rollie parked in a lot off 47th and Broadway and walked the four blocks to Knox's election headquarters on the first floor of a sixty-story high-rise office building. The headquarters had a separate entrance.

The headquarters interior was approximately eight thousand square feet with stations for about a hundred phones, but only a dozen were manned.

Posters of Knox and his family adorned the walks.

A woman in her thirties approached Rollie when he entered.

"May I help you, sir?" she said.

"I thought this place would be busier," Rollie said.

The woman smiled. "These are paid fund-raisers," she said. "Applications are being accepted for volunteers, of whom there will be hundreds within a few months."

"I was hoping to meet Mr. Knox," Rollie said. "I'd like to volunteer, you see."

"Mr. Knox is in Albany and won't be here for several weeks, but I'd be happy to give you a volunteer application," the woman said.

"That would be lovely," Rollie said.

CHAPTER TWELVE

Rollie sat at his desk in the office and studied a map of the New York Thruway.

It basically went from Queens north to Syracuse and west all the way to Buffalo. It spanned almost five hundred and seventy miles.

So, where did Knox go the night of September 17th?

Why such a hurry getting back that he got a speeding ticket?

He dumped the body.

Where?

Not on the side of the road; it would have been found and identified through fingerprints and dental records.

He buried the body.

But where?

He didn't pull off the road and bury her in the woods; that was too risky and Knox wasn't about risk. He was, as Mrs. Birmbaum said, a cold fish. Everything about him was carefully orchestrated.

He left that night with a specific destination in mind. And that could be anywhere on 570 miles of highway, or anywhere else.

That he was back within twenty-four house meant he didn't go too far.

Just far enough.

Say he left at midnight. How far could you drive with the corpse of your wife in the car?

One hour?

Two?

Three, tops.

A radius of one hundred and eighty miles from Manhattan. That would put you at your destination at around 3:00 am.

So, why the layover of twenty-four hours? It doesn't take that long to dig a grave. You dig the grave and head back to Manhattan the morning of the 17th.

He stayed overnight somewhere.

Why?

Rollie looked through his notes and documents again, searching for answers.

There weren't any.

He checked the time and called Teal, hoping he was still in his office.

"For Christ-sake, Rollie," Teal said.

"Knox's tax returns, can you get them?" Rollie said.

"Have you lost your fucking mind?" Teal said.

"He has to disclose them to the press anyway," Rollie said. "Or they will think he has something to hide."

"What are you looking for?" Teal said.

"I don't know. Something. Anything," Rollie said.

"I can't make that kind of request based upon 'something' and 'anything'," Teal said. "I need a goddamn valid reason."

"Can you at least check to see if he's disclosed them yet?" Rollie asked.

Teal sighed.

"Thanks, Bill," Rollie said.

After hanging up with Teal, Rollie went back and read some of the puff pieces on Knox again.

In one of the magazine articles, Knox spoke of his love for the outdoors, something bestowed on him by his father, James Knox. He spoke of hunting and fishing trips with his father as a boy.

James Knox passed away in 2010 from cancer.

Knox spoke of the loss of his father and how he still missed him to this day.

His love of the great outdoors.

Where?

"Hey, Dad. Dinner," Gloria said, poking her head in the office.

"Be right there," Rollie said.

After washing up in his bathroom, Rollie met the girls at the dinner table. They had gone through Georgia's cookbook again and found a recipe for lamb chops that was pretty good. Along with the chops, they had prepared roasted potatoes and carrots, and fresh baked rolls.

"Dad, we thought we could get ice cream for dessert again," Grace said.

"I don't see why not," Rollie said.

Dinner was finished by seven o'clock. "Dishes, and tidy up the kitchen, and we'll be off," Rollie said.

Rollie went to his office and combed through news articles. In at least six articles, Knox mentioned his love for the outdoors and how his father took him fishing and hunting.

The odd thing was Knox never mentioned one specific place where they fished and hunted. No mention of a favorite fishing hole or hunting spot, no tales of lodges and woods.

Nothing.

Nothing at all.

At 7:45, Grace stepped into the office. "Ready, Dad?"

•   •   •

It was a warm July night and the Dugout was crowded. After getting their baseball caps of ice-cream, they were lucky to find an empty bench.

"Mom would be glad we're still coming here," Gloria said.

"She would be," Rollie said.

"So, what's the real reason we're going to Florida?" Grace said.

"I need to follow up on this investigation and I thought I'd mix business with pleasure," Rollie said.

"Does this have anything to do with the lady who came to the house?" Grace said.

"Joanna Kearns? Yes, she is the client," Rollie said.

Gloria giggled.

"And we're giggling because…" Rollie said.

"Nothing, Dad," Grace said. "She thinks you should find a girlfriend."

"Three females in my life aren't enough?" Rollie said.

"We need a dog," Gloria said.

"No, we do not," Rollie said. "What we need is more ice cream."

•　　•　　•

Before turning in for the night, Rollie went to his desk and browsed the articles on Knox one more time.

Somebody somewhere had to know something about the great fisherman and hunter.

CHAPTER THIRTEEN

Holding a paper bag, Rollie met Hector in front of the building shortly before 11:00 a.m.

"I didn't remember anything new," Hector said.

"That's okay, I'm here to see Mrs. Birmbaum," Rollie said.

"I'll take you up," Hector said.

Rollie and Hector took the elevator up to the fifth floor where Hector knocked on Mrs. Birmbaum's door.

"Hello Hector," she said. "And Mr. Finch, I didn't expect to see you again."

"A few more questions came up. I hope you don't mind," Rollie said.

"Please come in," Mrs. Birmbaum said.

"I brought you this," Rollie said and gave the bag to her.

Mrs. Birmbaum opened the bag and removed a large container of Earl Grey Tea. "The good stuff," she said. "I'll make some. Hector, join us."

A few minutes later, Rollie, Hector, and Mrs. Birmbaum sat down at the kitchen table to tea for the second time.

"So what questions do you have for me?" Mrs. Birmbaum said.

"Just one, really," Rollie said. "When she was alive, do you remember Julia ever talking about John Knox fishing or hunting somewhere?"

"Just once, as I recall," Mrs. Birmbaum said. "It was before they had the baby. I was doing laundry down in the laundry room when Julia came down with a basket full of dirty clothes. She said they had just returned from a weekend of fishing at Knox's cabin in the Catskills. She told me she hated it, that she wasn't an outdoor girl."

"Can you remember where?" Rollie said.

"I don't think she ever told me," Mrs. Birmbaum said. "Just in the Catskills somewhere."

"And that was the only time?" Rollie said.

Mrs. Birmbaum nodded. "That I remember," she said.

"Thank you, Mrs. Birmbaum," Rollie said.

"And thank you for the tea," Mrs. Birmbaum said.

Hector went down to the street with Rollie.

"Thank you, Hector," Rollie said.

"So, I'm right, ain't I? This isn't a background check," Hector said.

. . .

Before entering the police station, Rollie picked up a dozen donuts.

"To what do I owe this honor," Teal said when Rollie set the donuts on his desk.

"Anything new on the tax returns?" Rollie said.

"Knox released the past six years," Teal said.

Rollie took a chair. "John Knox's father had a cabin in the Catskills," he said. "How do you get to the Catskills, Bill?"

"The New York Thruway," Teal said.

"I don't know where in the Catskills, but that makes sense," Rollie said.

"Do you how big the Catskills are?" Teal said.

"Twenty square miles," Rollie said.

"That big?"

"Which is why we have to find out *where* in the Catskills?"

"We?"

"*Mi casa, su casa,*" Rollie said.

Teal stood up. "I have a precinct commanders meeting at One PP," he said and removed two donuts from the bag.

"Call me at home later," Rollie said.

•　　•　　•

At his desk, Rollie studied a map of the Catskills. Twenty square miles is an area of four hundred miles.

The Catskills are located one hundred miles north of New York City.

Knox could have driven that in ninety minutes, buried the body, and driven back the same night.

But he stayed overnight.

Where? And why?

Rollie went to the kitchen for a cup of coffee. He looked out the kitchen window to the backyard. The girls were playing soccer. They were laughing and having a good time and safe from the John Knoxes of the world.

Rollie was lucky in that his daughters genuinely loved each other and the age differences didn't seem to matter to them at all. Soon to be eighteen, Grace loved the company of fifteen-year-old Giselle and thirteen-year-old Gloria more than her classmates from school.

Their mother instilled that, God bless her.

He returned to the office, sat at his desk, sipped coffee, and thought.

In all the articles where he speaks about his love of the outdoors, Knox never once mentioned a location.

He kept it a secret.

Because that's where the body is buried.

Around five o'clock, Teal called.

"How was your meeting?" Rollie said.

"Boring as hell," Teal said. "Good thing I had two donuts to keep me occupied."

"And Knox?"

"I tried, but except for the six years he's released, the rest are sealed," Teal said.

"He's hiding something," Rollie said.

"Unless a judge agrees to let us take a peek, there isn't much we can do about it," Teal said. "And I have zero cause to ask a judge."

"Can you check and find out when the last time Knox applied for a hunting and fishing permit?" Rollie said.

"That won't tell us where the location of his cabin is," Teal said.

"No, but it might tell us the last time he used it," Rollie said.

"Always one step ahead of me, aren't you?" Teal said.

"I have more time to sit around and think than you do," Rollie said.

"I'll check with fish and game in the morning and call you with the results," Teal said.

"Thanks, Bill," Rollie said.

After hanging up with Teal, Rollie searched for places to fish and hunt in the Catskills. There were hundreds of them.

Without a specific location, Knox's secret would remain just that, a secret.

Grace knocked on the office door, opened it and poked her head in. "We're going to start dinner now. Any requests?"

"How about a couple of large pizzas?" Rollie said.

"How about yes," Grace said.

"Order them from The Roma and I'll pick them up," Rollie said.

"Thanks, Dad," Grace said.

• • •

"Three days and we're in Florida," Grace said as she bit into a slice of pizza.

"Forty days and we're back in school," Gloria said.

"That reminds me," Rollie said. "Grace, any ides of where you want to go to college?"

"A week before school starts, I have to meet with my guidance counselor about that," Grace said.

"What did you carry last year, A Minus?" Rollie said.

Grace nodded.

"Make that straight As, and any college you want is yours," Rollie said.

"I have some ideas I'll talk to you about later," Grace said.

• • •

After dinner, Rollie took a mug of coffee to the backyard. Grace came out a few minutes later with a can of ginger ale.

She sat beside him at the patio table.

"So Dad, I was thinking of following in your footsteps," Grace said.

"Become a police officer?" Rollie said.

"No, join the Army like you did," Grace said. "When I get out, I can get a VA loan for college like you did."

Oh dear God, Rollie thought.

"I did it backwards," Rollie said.

"How do you mean?" Grace said.

"I should have gone to college first, and then I could have gone in as an officer," Rollie said. "Instead of a private. You don't want to be a private."

"I don't?"

"Not when you can be an officer," Rollie said.

"An officer?"

"Even a junior officer makes a lot more money than a private," Rollie said. "And think of how great Lieutenant or Captain Grace Finch would look on a resume," Rollie said.

"I guess."

"Trust me."

After Grace went inside, Rollie wiped his brow. "That, hopefully, bought me four years," he said.

CHAPTER FOURTEEN

"Dad, can we go tanning today?" Grace said. "We'd like to get a base coat, so we don't fry in Florida."

"Why don't you actually go to the beach? I'll let you take the car."

Grace smiled. Letting her take the Buick was Rollie's way of telling her she was out of the doghouse for the Gloria-makeup incident at the movies.

"Be right back," Grace said.

She left the office, and Rollie continued surfing the internet for any and all information about John Knox.

Once he became lieutenant governor, he became a New York media darling. Not since Kennedy had there been such a beautiful couple in politics as John and Dana Knox.

Together with their good-looking kids, every article dripped with the idea of Knox as the next governor to become president. And why not? There hasn't been a governor from New York in the White House since FDR. The country was due.

Grace returned. "We're going to leave at one o'clock today," she said.

"The car keys are on the kitchen counter," Rollie said. "And Grace..."

"I know," Grace said. "Responsibility."

After the girls left, Rollie found an article written just a few weeks ago.

The article was titled "Twenty Questions with the Next Governor." Why not just anoint the man with holy water and call it good? Rollie thought.

However, the article proved useful. One question was, "How did you cope with the death of your first wife?"

Knox's answer was a self-congratulatory testimonial to himself, describing how he fell into despair, and then fought his way back with the help of family, friends, and counseling.

Knox said that the experience of losing his wife gave him the strength and understanding to cope with losing his father just a few years later in 2006, and his mother the year after that.

And of course, the silver lining was new love and his second wife, Dana.

The piece was enough to give you sugar-shock.

Rollie went to the kitchen to refill his cup of coffee and when he returned to his desk, Teal called on the hard line.

"Spring of 2001 was the last time Knox applied for a fishing and hunting license," Teal said.

"The great hunter and outdoorsman is a fraud," Rollie said.

"I can't arrest a man for *not* fishing," Teal said.

"I need those tax returns," Rollie said.

"And I need a bloody steak," Teal said.

"Come to dinner when we get back from Florida, and I'll cook you one," Rollie said.

"I like this sharing attitude," Teal said.

After hanging up with Teal, Rollie changed into sweats and did an hour on the step climber.

Knox hadn't fished or hunted in nearly twenty years, yet he bragged about his love of the great outdoors.

Was there anything about the man that was real?

· · ·

The girls came back close to dinnertime. They had a reddish glow to their skin.

"We're going to play soccer in the backyard," Grace said.

Rollie was in his office finishing up some notes on another case.

He thought back to the time after his wife died. He had retired from the job a few years earlier to take care of her, and after she passed, there was a great void in his life.

To ease the pain and fill the void, he concentrated on what made him happy, his three daughters, and what occupied his time, work as a private investigator.

Supposedly a great outdoorsman, Knox never returned to the outdoors as a diversion for him or his daughter.

Why?

The answer lies in the Catskills.

And possibly in his tax returns.

CHAPTER FIFTEEN

Their flight left LaGuardia Airport at 11:10 and touched down in Orlando at 1:45. While the girls monitored the luggage, Rollie rented a full-size sedan and met them curbside.

Rollie programmed the GPS to take them to the Universal Resort Hotel and they arrived about thirty minutes later.

As he checked them in, the girls were blown away by the sights and sounds of the lavish resort.

Their suite on the fourteenth floor had four bedrooms and a living room. By the time they unpacked and met in the living room, it was close to four o'clock.

"Dad, we want to hit the pool," Grace said.

Rollie and the girls went down to the massive, split-level pool that featured a small waterfall and all manner of colored lights after dark.

As the girls swam and splashed in the pool, Rollie called Joanna Kearns.

"Rollie, are you in Orlando?" she said.

"As promised."

"My mother wants to make us lunch, so come around noon, okay?"

"All I need is the address," Rollie said.

He wrote it down in his ever-present notebook.

"I'll be there at noon," Rollie said.

As he hung up, Rollie noticed a boy of about eighteen moving in on Giselle. Grace and Gloria were splashing about nearby.

Rollie was about to stand up when Grace swam over to the boy and spoke to him. The boy nodded and took off.

"Big sister to the rescue," Rollie said.

By six o'clock, the girls were starving. After showers and changes of clothes, they opted for one of the hotel dining rooms.

The agenda for the girls for the next day was to visit Universal, an all-day affair. Tickets were included in the package trip, but Rollie still had to part with two hundred dollars in spending money for the girls.

•   •   •

With the girls on their way by ferry to Universal, Rollie re-read his notebook and left the hotel at 11:15 to see Joanna's mother.

The GPS guided him right to the doorstep of her townhouse.

Joanna answered the door. "Rollie, come in," she said. "Mom is in the kitchen. Her name is Janice."

Rollie followed Joanna to the kitchen where Janice was preparing lunch.

"Mother, this is Rollie Finch," Joanna said.

Janice was seventy-five-years-old, but could pass for sixty. She smiled at Rollie and said, "Please sit down, lunch in ten minutes."

Rollie and Joanna took chairs at the table, and Janice poured coffee.

"Mr. Finch, that no-good-bastard killed my daughter and has gotten away with it all these years," Janice said.

"Mother, please," Joanna said.

"Well, I'm sorry, but it burns me up inside," Janice said.

"Mrs. Kearns, for what it's worth, I believe that John Knox killed your daughter," Rollie said.

Janice looked at Rollie. "You do?" she said.

"Yes, but proving it is another matter," Rollie said. "Mrs. Kearns, tell me about John Knox."

"Well, I was against the marriage from the start," Janice said. "But Julia was young and couldn't see past his good looks. She couldn't see he was a complete phony."

"How do you mean?" Rollie said.

"He was such a reptile," Janice said. "You could see he practiced his smile in front of a mirror. When he spoke, it was never from the heart. His blue eyes were always cold, never warm. The eyes tell you all you need to know about a person, right?"

"Mrs. Kearns, did…?" Rollie said.

"Janice, please."

Rollie nodded. "Janice, did your daughter ever talk about going to the Catskills with Knox?"

"Yes. Julia wasn't an outdoor girl, I'm afraid," Janice said. "John had this cabin he inherited from his father on a lake somewhere. She hated it and only went once or maybe twice."

"Do you know where this cabin is located?" Rollie said.

"Let me think," Janice said. "Wait."

Janice stood up and dashed off to her bedroom. She returned a few minutes later with a white tee-shirt. "This was one of the last things Julie ever gave me," she said and held up the tee-shirt.

The front read, "I Went To Andes And Lived To Tell About It."

Rollie nodded. "Thank you," he said.

"The bread," Janice said.

Janice removed a loaf of break from the oven and set it on the counter to cool.

"How much did she confide in you?" Rollie said.

"A great deal," Janice said. "With her sister, too."

"Did she ever discuss getting a divorce?" Rollie said.

"Oh, yes. Many times," Janice said. "Almost to the day she was killed."

Janice stood up and sliced the fresh bread into thick slices and made warm roast beef sandwiches and hot French fries she fried in olive oil.

Rollie took a bite of his sandwich. It was wonderful.

"Janice, after you heard about the World Trade Center, you called Julia at home?" Rollie said.

"A dozen times or more," Janice said. "Twenty years ago, most people still didn't have cell phones. Her home number was all she had. Around 11:30 or so, John answered the phone. He sounded disheveled, sleepy. I told him what happened. He turned the TV on and started screaming and hung up. It was all an act, if you ask me."

They finished their sandwiches and chatted some more until Rollie said, "Thank you, Janice, for a wonderful lunch, and all the information."

"You'll be staying with this, then?" Janice said.

"Yes."

"We can't expect you to work for free," Janice said and nodded to Joanna.

Joanna reached into her handbag and produced a check for five thousand dollars and gave it to Rollie.

"We really want you to put him where he belongs," Janice said.

"I'll walk you out," Joanna said.

At the car, Rollie said, "Why don't you have dinner with me and the girls tonight?"

"I don't want to intrude," Joanna said.

"It will be fun, and it's only thirty minutes away," Rollie said. "Meet us in the lobby at 6:00."

Joanna nodded.

"Good. See you at 6:00," Rollie said.

•   •   •

In his hotel room, Rollie did a search for Andes, New York.

Andes was a tiny town in Delaware County in New York State. It was home to a small lake called Big Pond. It was also home to a dozen species of fish, and tournaments were held every year.

The town and lake were accessible by Route 28 off the New York Thruway.

About ninety minutes each way, yet he stayed overnight.

Around four o'clock, Rollie took a shower and changed into casual dinner clothes. Then he went down to the lobby and called Teal on his cell phone.

"I thought you were in Florida," Teal said.

"I am," Rollie said. "I just wanted to see if you had any luck on Knox's tax returns yet."

"Nope. When are you seeing Timmons?"

"Day after tomorrow," Rollie said. "Bill, you ever go fishing?"

"What am I, a mountain man now?" Teal said.

"I'll take that as a no."

"A couple of times as a kid off the pier at Coney Island."

"Maybe we'll go when I get home," Rollie said.

"I wouldn't bet on it."

"I'll call you after I see Timmons," Rollie said.

The girls showed up at 5:30.

"Go change for dinner, I'll wait for you here," Rollie told them.

The girls returned at six o'clock, in their new clothes, and wearing their new perfumes.

"Where are we going?" Grace said.

"The veranda, if that's okay with you three," Rollie said.

"Sure," Grace said.

"We can hit the pool afterward," Giselle said.

"What are we waiting for?" Gloria said.

Rollie nodded at the lobby doors. "Her," he said.

The girls looked at Joanna and rushed to her side. Joanna was equally as delighted to see them.

The girls wasted no time telling Joanna about Universal.

"Tomorrow is Disney," Gloria said.

"Why don't you join us?" Grace said.

"I couldn't," Joanna said.

"Dad?" Grace said.

"If you have nothing else to do tomorrow, we'd be happy to have you join us," Rollie said.

Joanna nodded. "Okay," she said. "But I'll buy my own ticket."

After dinner, the girls changed and went to the pool. Rollie and Joanna sat poolside in lounge chairs.

"They are wonderful girls," Joanna said.

"You can thank their mother for that," Rollie said.

"You seem to have done pretty well with them," Joanna said.

"Their mother laid a good foundation," Rollie said.

"My two left the nest a few years back," Joanna said. "It was a big adjustment. Then when my husband died, I was never so lonely in all my life."

"I know the feeling," Rollie said.

Joanna sighed. "Do you think you can catch him, Rollie?"

"I'm sure as hell going to try," Rollie said.

"We haven't paid you enough for…" Joanna said.

"If I need more, I'll ask," Rollie said. "Otherwise, don't worry about it. Okay?"

"It's getting late," Joanna said. "If you want me to go with you tomorrow, I'll need my beauty sleep tonight."

"Girls, come say goodnight to Joanna," Rollie said.

After hugs all around, Rollie walked Joanna to her car. "Ten o'clock?" Rollie said.

"See you then," Joanna said.

Rollie returned to the pool. "Girls, thirty minutes," he said.

CHAPTER SIXTEEN

The day at Disney World passed quickly. There was so much to see and do and eat that by six o'clock, the girls were exhausted.

They took the water ferry back to the hotel where the girls said goodnight to Joanna and went up to their suite.

Rollie and Joanna sat on a sofa in the lobby for a while.

"When do you head back to South Carolina?" Rollie said.

"A couple of days," Joanna said. "I have a garden to tend to, and the first of August, I have a school board meeting."

"I'll call you after I meet with Timmons," Rollie said.

Joanna nodded. "I wish you had been the detective I went to back then," she said.

"I don't know if it would have made a difference," Rollie said. "The city was in pretty bad shape at that time."

Joanna nodded. "Sad, isn't it? That a man could use 9/11 to get away with murder."

"Just keep in mind there is no statute of limitations on murder," Rollie said.

Joanna smiled. "I guess I'd better head back to my mother's place," she said.

"I'll walk you to your car," Rollie said.

•　　•　　•

After breakfast, Rollie checked out of the hotel and drove southeast to the Florida Keys. The distance was around four hundred miles. They stopped once for lunch and arrived at their resort on Islamorada Key around 4:00 in the afternoon.

The girls had never seen anything like the Keys, the longest string of islands connected by bridges in the world.

After checking in, the girls hit the pool while Rollie watched from a lounge chair.

What would he do if someone came along and murdered one of his daughters? Would he take the civilized route and allow the law to take its course?

Or would he allow guttural instincts to get the better of him?

That was a question for another day.

"Girls, it's six o'clock. Let's get ready for dinner," Rollie said.

They ate at a local restaurant that bragged it was the birth place of the Key Lime Pie.

When they returned to their suite, Rollie said, "After breakfast, we'll got to the park at 10:00 when it opens. I'll get tickets for you to swim with dolphins, and then I have to do some work, but I'll be back in time to watch you swim."

While the girls went to bed, Rollie stayed up for a bit and thought about Al Timmons.

Their paths had crossed several times when Rollie was a patrolman and more frequently when Rollie made detective. Although they never worked a case together, Rollie knew Timmons was a solid detective, one who never just went through the motions on a case.

Rollie wondered how Timmons would react to the surprise visit.

• • •

"Alright, girls, have a good time," Rollie said.

"You'll be back to watch us swim?" Grace said.

"Promise," Rollie said. "Do a check before you go in. Tickets?"

"I have them," Grace said.

"Tickets to swim with the dolphins?" Rollie said.

"Got 'em," Grace said.

"Spending money?" Rollie said.

"Wait," Grace said and went through her handbag. "Eleven dollars and loose change."

Rollie removed five twenty-dollar bills from his wallet and gave them to Grace.

"Have fun, I'll see you before 2:00," he said.

Rollie programmed the GPS in the rental car to take him to No Name Key where Timmons owned a house near the water.

The drive took about twenty minutes.

When Rollie arrived, Timmons was on the front porch of a small house that was in dire need of paint and a lawn-mowing.

As he walked up the steps of the porch, Rollie saw that Timmons was hooked up to an oxygen tank.

"Al Timmons?" Rollie said.

"Who wants to know?" Timmons said.

"Detective Rollie Finch," Rollie said.

Timmons sat up straight and removed the nose clips from his nostrils. "No kidding?" he said. "Come on up here."

Rollie went up the porch. "How are you, Al?" he said.

"Aching for a cigarette. Got any?" Timmons said.

"I don't think you should be smoking," Rollie said. "What do you have?"

"COPD." Timmons replaced the nose clips. "So, what brings you to the beautiful Keys, Rollie?"

"See you."

"About?"

"John Knox," Rollie said.

Timmons looked at Rollie and slowly smiled. "The next governor of New-fucking-York. What about him?"

"I read all your case files on him," Rollie said.

"Why?"

"I'm private now," Rollie said. "I've been hired by the family of Julie Knox to investigate her death."

"Twenty years after the fact?" Timmons asked.

"So, what did you leave out of your reports?" Rollie said.

"What makes you think I left something out?" Timmons said.

"Come on, Al, let's not bullshit each other," Rollie said.

"Got any cigarettes?"

"I don't smoke."

"Get me a pack, and I'll tell you what I left out," Timmons said.

"I don't think that's a good idea," Rollie said.

"I turn the tank off when I smoke," Timmons said. "One pack of Camels, unfiltered, for my information."

"Be right back," Rollie said.

Rollie drove a few blocks to Route 1, found a convenience store, bought a pack of Camels and asked for a book of matches. Then he drove back to Timmons's house, went up to the porch and handed the cigarettes and matches to Timmons.

"For God's sake, turn off the tank before you blow us both up," Rollie said.

"Grab us a couple of cold sodas from the fridge, Rollie," Timmons said.

Rollie went inside and returned with two cans of Coke and gave one to Timmons, who had lit a cigarette in the meantime. "Tank's off," he said, "Relax."

Rollie took a sip of Coke. "So?" he said.

"I know the son of a bitch killed her," Timmons said, "but no judge would give me a warrant after 9/11. They were too busy hiding under their benches. I went to the captain and asked him if he could do something. Next thing I know, I'm called before the Chief of D's."

"Who was that at the time?" Rollie said.

"Pearly," Timmons said. "Sam Pearly. Know what he said to me? He said I needed to drop the case. Said the city couldn't afford a scandal like that so soon after 9/11."

"And you said?"

"I told him we'd be letting a murderer get away with murder."

"And he said?"

"He asked me if I was looking forward to one day receiving my pension," Timmons said. "I had eighteen years in at the time. I did what I was ordered to do."

"What made you think Knox was guilty?" Rollie said.

"I timed her right from her apartment to Chambers Street," Timmons said. "It took me forty-six minutes. Even if she left her apartment right after hanging up with her sister, she wouldn't have reached Chambers Street until thirty minutes after the plane hit the first tower."

"And Pearly didn't care?" Rollie said.

"He gave me a direct order to drop the whole fucking thing," Timmons said. "I felt terrible for her sister and family, but there was nothing I could do after that."

"Gotta love the brass," Rollie said.

"And now you're working on it privately?" Timmons said.

"With a little help from Bill Teal," Rollie said.

"He's a captain now, right? Or so I've heard."

Rollie nodded.

"Make any headway?"

"Some. Not enough."

"I put in thirty years, Rollie," Timmons said. "It's the only case I ever tanked."

Rollie nodded.

"If you need anything, call me," Timmons said.

"I just might, Al," Rollie said.

"Thanks for the smokes," Timmons said.

.   .   .

Rollie drove to the Theatre of the Sea and called Teal from the parking lot.

"Did you see Timmons?" Teal said.

"I just left him," Rollie said.

"And he said?"

"Timmons said the Chief of D's told him to drop the case," Rollie said.

Teal was silent for a moment. "The Chief of Detectives told him that?"

"I believe him," Rollie said. "He clocked the trip to the Trade Center towers at forty-six minutes, same as me. He had eighteen in at the time, and his pension was threatened if he didn't shelve it."

"Who was Chief of D's at that time?" Teal said.

"Pearly."

"That fucking asshole," Teal said. "He was fired in 2003 for misuse of funds and manpower."

"I remember," Rollie said. "See if you can find out where he is now."

"When are you coming home?"

"Day after tomorrow."

"I'll see what I can do," Teal said.

After hanging up, Rollie entered the Theater of the Sea and

walked to the lagoon where swimming with dolphins was allowed.

The girls were with a group of six others that were taking instructions from a trainer. Rollie came up behind them and they turned around.

"Dad," Grace said.

"I'll be right over there on the observation deck," Rollie said.

He went to the deck with others there to watch and set his camera on his phone to video. On their honeymoon, Rollie and Georgia came to the Keys, and Georgia also swam with the dolphins.

When it was their turn to swim, Grace went first. She swam out to the edge of the lagoon and waited for the dolphin to swim to her, then Grace held its fin and the dolphin took her for a ride.

Giselle went next, followed by Gloria.

Afterward, the girls bubbled over with excitement talking about their swims. They talked about it on the way back to the hotel and again in the car as Rollie drove them south to Key West.

Finally, Grace said, "Dad, where are we going?"

"Dinner," Rollie said.

When they reached Key West, Rollie parked in a lot and took the girls to the famous boardwalk. Thousands of people were about, including street musicians, dancers, and acrobats.

They stopped at the famous sign that read "90 miles to Cuba" and the Hemingway House before Rollie led them to a restaurant.

"Dad, this place is full of cats," Grace said

A hostess took them to a courtyard table. Several cats showed up as soon as they were seated.

"As the story goes, these cats are all descendants of Hemmingway's famous six-toed cats," Rollie said.

"Should we feed them?" Gloria said.

"You're expected to," Rollie said.

They ordered chicken, and tiny bits of food managed to find

their way to a dozen cats.

After dinner, Rollie led them back to the boardwalk to watch the sun set over the ocean. Thousands of people stopped whatever they were doing to watch the magnificent sight of the Key West sunset.

As Rollie drove them back to the hotel, Gloria said, "This was the best time ever."

CHAPTER SEVENTEEN

Rollie parked in the lot on 47th and Broadway, and walked to Knox's campaign headquarters on 51st Street.

Knox was in, and the headquarters buzzed with excitement. Hundreds of people filled the room.

The same woman Rollie spoke to weeks ago approached him.

"Volunteer?" she said.

"Rollie Finch to see Mr. Knox," Rollie said.

"Do you have an appointment?"

Rollie gave her his business card. "Mr. Knox will see me," he said.

The woman looked at the card, frowned, and walked to a door marked 'private,' opened it, went inside, and closed it behind her. She was gone several minutes and when she emerged, she was accompanied by a very large and sinister-looking man wearing a suit.

"Can I help you?" he said.

"Are you John Knox?" Rollie said.

"No."

"Then you can't," Rollie said.

The man grinned at Rollie. "Follow me," he said.

Rollie followed the man into an office where Knox sat behind a cluttered desk. Knox was holding Rollie's business card.

Knox looked at Rollie as the man in the suit stood against the wall.

"Mr. Finch, what is your business with me?" Knox said.

"Nothing complicated," Rollie said. "You murdered your first wife on 9/11, and I've been hired to investigate."

Knox stared at Rollie. For a moment, his blue eyes turned black, then stormy, then they lightened and he grinned his boyish grin.

"I was wondering when her sister was going to pop up," Knox said.

"I'm not at liberty to reveal my client," Rollie said.

"Go back and tell your client I didn't kill my wife," Knox said. "She died in Tower One on the 81st floor."

"So says you," Rollie said. "Evidence says otherwise."

The man against the wall started to walk toward Rollie and Knox waved him off.

"What evidence?" Knox said. "Everything was looked at twenty years ago and dismissed."

"There are no statutes of limitations on murder," Rollie said. "You're a lawyer, you know that."

"Except nobody was murdered," Knox said. "Julia died in Tower One."

"How?" Rollie said.

"What do you mean, how?" Knox said. "Terrorists flew a fucking 767 into the 86th floor, that's how."

"That's not the 'how' that I mean," Rollie said. "I mean how did she hang up with her sister at 8:27 a.m. and be in Tower One on the 81st floor eighteen minutes later. *That* 'how'."

"They must have made a mistake on the time," Knox said.

"I have the phone bill. The call lasted from 8:15 until 8:27. No mistake," Rollie said.

Knox stared at Rollie. "She died on 9/11 on the 81st floor of Tower One," he said. "And that's all there is to it. If you've gotten mixed up with her crazy family and have come here to make me relive the worst moment in my life, then congratulations."

"Did she grow wings? Ride a magic carpet? How did she get there in eighteen minutes when it's at least a forty minute trip door-to-door?" Rollie said.

"I think we're through here," Knox said.

"On the contrary, I'm just getting warmed up," Rollie said. "You told the police you slept until 11:30 that day, that you were sick."

"I had some bad fish the night before," Knox said. "I had a touch of food poisoning and I slept late."

"So much that you didn't hear the phone ringing for three hours?" Rollie said.

"I was asleep," Knox said. "Karl, would you show Mr. Finch the door? Mr. Finch, I have work to do."

Rollie turned and walked to the door that Karl held open.

"We'll talk again," Rollie said. "Soon."

"Don't count on it," Knox said.

Rollie left the headquarters and walked along Broadway to the garage on 47th Street. He didn't need to look back to know that Karl was on his tail.

Rollie entered the garage, immediately exited on 46th Street and ducked into a coffee shop across the street.

He watched through the window as Karl entered the garage. Fifteen minutes later, Karl returned to the street and walked back toward Knox's headquarters.

"And away we go," Rollie said.

•   •   •

"Bill, Rollie," Rollie said when Teal answered his phone. "I'm outside the precinct. Got a few minutes?"

"Did you…?" Teal said.

"A dozen, and still warm," Rollie said.

"In that case, I have a few minutes," Teal said.

Rollie went into the station to Teal's office and set the bag on his desk. "I also picked up two coffees," Rollie said.

Rollie opened his coffee and sat in a chair. "Sam Pearly?"

"He's eighty-one now and living in a retirement community in South Carolina," Teal said.

"I'll need address and phone number," Rollie said.

Teal bit into a donut and washed it down with a sip of coffee.

"He did it, Bill," Rollie said. "Knox killed his wife."

"Suppose he did, how did he do it, and where is the body?" Teal said.

"I don't know, but I looked into his eyes and…"

"When? When did you look into his eyes?"

"Not an hour ago," Rollie said. "I spoke to him at his headquarters on Broadway. He sent a goon to follow me to my car, but I ditched him."

"He'll make some calls," Teal said. "He'll have the governor and state's attorney squash this like a bug and you along with it."

"No he won't," Rollie said. "He won't want the publicity of a scandal so close to the election."

"How far did you go?" Teal said.

"I told him he killed his wife," Rollie said. "I wanted to gage his reaction."

"And?"

"I saw it in his eyes. He did it," Rollie said.

"Too bad you can't subpoena his eyes," Teal said. "Are you going to see Pearly?"

"In a few days," Rollie said. "I have a few things to do first."

"Rollie, this is getting ugly," Teal said.

"That's what murder is."

. . .

After dinner, Rollie had the girls sit on the sofa in the living room while he inserted a disc into the DVD player.

Rollie took his easy chair while the girls watched themselves swim with a dolphin in the lagoon at the Theater of the Sea.

"Oh my God, look at me," Grace said. "And Giselle and Gloria."

Rollie stood up. "I showed you that, so I can show you this," he said.

He removed the disc and inserted another, and then took his seat again.

Georgia filled the television. She was wearing a blue racing bathing suit and she waved at the camera.

"Mom was so beautiful," Grace said.

The camera panned to show the lagoon at the Theater of the Sea.

"That's where we were!" Giselle said.

The camera cut to Georgia in the lagoon, waving to Rollie. Then to her swimming with a dolphin.

When it ended, the girls were in tears.

"I took that on our honeymoon," Rollie said.

"Can we watch it again?" Grace said.

"As much as you like," Rollie said. He went to the kitchen for a can of ginger ale, and took it the backyard and sat at the patio table.

After a while, Grace joined him. She didn't say anything but gave him a long hug. Rollie told her how proud of her he was for her being so responsible in Florida. He asked if he could put her in charge tomorrow as well. "Yes," she said, continuing her hug.

CHAPTER EIGHTEEN

In the morning, Rollie drove to the building where the Registry of Deeds was located in Delaware County about one hundred miles north of Manhattan.

There were a few clerks on hand to assist people, but Rollie preferred to keep his business private. Most of the people doing title searches were real estate agents, so Rollie fit right in as he riffled through records.

It took a while, but finally he located the purchase of a cabin on Big Pond Lake in the town of Andes by James Francis Knox in 1966.

The 1966 price was eleven thousand dollars.

In 2007, Knox sold the property for eighty thousand, a tidy profit.

Maybe that's what he didn't want people to see on his tax returns, that the great hunter and fisherman sold his fishing cabin.

Rollie made a copy of the documents before leaving the building and heading to his car. He programmed the GPS, stopped for coffee, and then headed to Big Pond Lake in the town of Andes.

The ride took about thirty minutes. The cabin was off a dirt road. The front faced the lake, the rear faced thick woodlands made up of pine and birch trees.

Rollie parked on the road and walked down to the front of the cabin. The new owners had put in some considerable work and money in refurbishing the place. There was a dock and a pontoon boat in the water.

No one was home.

Rollie walked back to his car, crossed the road, and entered the woods. Within twenty yards, the woods were so dense almost all sunlight was blocked by the trees. He turned around and walked back to his car.

Knox drove up at night and stayed in the cabin until the following day. After dark, he carried the body into the woods, buried her, and covered the grave with brush and shrubs, concealing it from any hikers or hunters. He drove back to Manhattan after that, and got a speeding ticket on the Thruway for his troubles.

Twenty years later, the grave is part of the landscape.

After his father died, Knox sold the cabin, ending all ties to the wife he murdered.

Rollie drove around for a bit and found a diner in the tiny town of Andes. He went in, took a booth by the window, and ordered a chicken breast sandwich with thick cut fries and a glass of ginger ale.

As he ate, he studied the dozens of framed photographs hanging on the walls. One caught his attention and he stood to look at it. The photograph was from a fishing tournament held on Big Pond Lake in 1998.

James and John Knox grinned for the camera as they held up a prize-winning rainbow trout.

After lunch, Rollie drove home and was as his desk in time to catch Teal at the office.

"Bill, I located the Knox cabin in the Catskills," Rollie said. "It's on Big Pond Lake, and behind it is woods so thick sunlight doesn't penetrate the trees."

"Big Pond, that's an oxymoron like jumbo shrimp," Teal said.

"Never mind the oxymoron, Knox drove the body to Big Pond and buried her in the woods," Rollie said.

"Got proof?"

"Not yet."

"Then all you got is a theory, just like Einstein," Teal said.

"He sold it in 2007, ending his ties to it, and that's what he doesn't want to be seen on his 2008 tax returns," Rollie said. "He likes to brag about what a great outdoorsman he is and keep it generic. When I saw him the other day, his face hasn't seen the sun in years."

"We have the phone bill, the speeding ticket, and what else?" Teal said.

"How about a trip to the country?" Rollie said.

"What for?

"A free lunch."

"When?"

"As soon as I get back from seeing Pearly."

"It better be some lunch," Teal said.

After hanging up with Teal, Rollie called the airlines and reserved a round trip ticket to South Carolina.

At dinner, he told the girls.

"I'll be leaving at 6:00 tomorrow morning, and I won't be home until around 9:00," he said. "Do I need to hire a baby-sitter for the day?"

"No, Dad, you don't," Grace said.

"Believe me, Grace is tougher on us than you are," Gloria said. "Compared to her, you're a softie."

Grace and Giselle glared at Gloria.

"Oops," Gloria said.

CHAPTER NINETEEN

Rollie's plane touched down at 9:40 in the morning.. Having no luggage except his briefcase, he whisked directly to the rental car booth and rented a car for the day.

After programming the GPS to take him to the home of Sam Pearly, Rollie stopped once for coffee on the three-hour drive.

South Carolina was a beautiful state, but Rollie's mind was only on seeing Sam Pearly.

Before leaving home, Rollie did his homework. Almost from the start, Pearly was destined to become an administrator.

He wasn't a good cop or detective, but in an administrative capacity, he was outstanding and slowly rose up the ranks. He served as Chief of Detectives from 1992 until 2003, when, after he was asked to retire early by the police chief and he refused, Pearly was terminated with full pension and benefits on a bogus charge of misuse of funds.

The truth was that a new police chief wanted his own people, and he felt Pearly was loyal to the old administration.

That's politics.

After three hours of driving, Rollie arrived at Pearly's condo in a large retirement village just outside the town of Goose Creek.

A woman of about fifty answered the door.

"Yes?" she said.

"Detective Rollie Finch, NYPD, to see Mr. Pearly," Rollie said.

"I'm his daughter," the woman said. "My father had his chemo treatment yesterday and isn't feeling very…"

"Let him in," Pearly called from behind the door.

The woman opened the door and Rollie entered.

Sam Pearly was dressed in pajamas and a robe, and was seated on the sofa. He was thin and gaunt looking, a sick man.

"Bring Mr. Finch some coffee, will you sweetheart?" Pearly said. "Me, too."

The woman nodded and went to the kitchen.

"Have a seat Mr. Finch and tell me what I can do to help New York's finest," Pearly said.

"I've reopened an old case," Rollie said. "I'd…"

The daughter returned with two cups of coffee, gave one to Pearly and the other to Rollie.

"Thank you, dear," Pearly said. "My daughter is staying with me while I undergo chemo treatments for liver cancer. It's fifty-fifty, so the doctors say."

"I'm sorry to hear that," Rollie said.

"So, what were you saying about an old case?" Pearly said.

"Do you know who John Knox is?" Rollie said.

"That prick running for New York governor," Pearly said.

"That's right, but he's also suspected of killing his wife on 9/11," Rollie said. "Detective Al Timmons worked the case, and he was told to close it by you. Do you remember that?"

Pearly nodded. "That order came from the top to pause that investigation. Directly from the commissioner," he said.

"Why?" Rollie said.

"He felt the city couldn't afford such a sandal so soon after the Twin Towers fell," Pearly said. "Remember how it was then?"

Rollie nodded.

"He felt, why make it worse," Pearly said.

"And how did you feel?" Rollie said.

"After reviewing the facts, I felt Knox just might be guilty," Pearly said.

"You told that to the commissioner?" Rollie said.

"Yes. Even showed him the reports from Timmons," Pearly said. "He told me to wait an appropriate amount of time and reopen it. Then a new administration took over, sent my ass packing, and it got lost in the system."

Rollie drank some coffee. It was quite good.

"So, what's your interest in the twenty-year-old Knox case?" Pearly said.

"I retired from the homicide squad after my wife died," Rollie said. "I'm private now, and the family of Knox's wife hired me to investigate him."

"And how is that coming along?" Pearly said.

"I believe he did it," Rollie said. "I don't know if I can prove it, but I know that he did it."

"If you don't, that prick will ride Albany right into the White House," Pearly said.

"I'm afraid you're right about that," Rollie said.

"Ya know, when they kicked me out, my pension was a hundred and five thousand a year plus full benefits," Pearly said. "It's up to one twenty a year now. I won't live much longer. Everything I have goes to my daughter. If you could nail this bastard, I will die a content man."

"Can you do me a favor?" Rollie said.

"If it doesn't require longevity," Pearly said.

"Can you write a letter to the police commissioner requesting him to officially reopen the Knox case?" Rollie said.

"I don't know what good that would do, but I'll write your letter," Pearly said.

.   .   .

While he waited for his flight, Rollie sat in a chair outside his terminal and read Pearly's hand-written letter.

It was addressed to the police commissioner and was nearly three pages in length. Pearly explained in the text how he thought Detective Al Timmons had enough evidence to obtain a warrant, but the police commissioner at that time ordered the case closed.

Pearly ended the letter by asking the commissioner to please request to have the case officially reopened.

If nothing else, the letter would make Al Timmons happy.

Rollie was home in time to have dinner with the girls.

CHAPTER TWENTY

Rollie drove to Manhattan, parked in the garage on West 47th Street, walked to 51st and Broadway, and waited across the street from Knox's headquarters for Knox to arrive.

He grabbed a coffee and a soft pretzel, munching and sipping while he waited. Around 10:45, Knox's limo arrived and pulled curbside.

Knox, Karl, and another aide got out and entered the campaign headquarters.

Rollie finished his pretzel and coffee, waiting until 11:15 to call Knox on his cell phone.

"Rollie Finch for Mr. Knox," Rollie told the girl that answered the phone. "He'll take my call."

After being on hold for less than a minute, Knox came on the line. "You have exactly thirty seconds," he said. "Starting now."

"I have a letter you should see," Rollie said.

"From whom to whom?" Knox said.

"The retired Chief of New York City Detectives to the Police Commissioner of New York requesting the case against you for murder be reopened," Rollie said.

Knox was silent, but Rollie could hear his deep breathing.

"It's well-written," Rollie said. "I thought you might be interested in having a copy to show your lawyers."

"Where are you?" Knox said.

"Right across the street," Rollie said.

"Karl will see you to my office," Knox said and hung up.

Rollie crossed the street in time for Karl to appear at the door. Karl was even taller than Knox, and he grinned down at Rollie as he approached.

"If it isn't the little man," Karl said.

"I admit I'm no idiot giant like yourself," Rollie said.

"Follow me, laughing boy," Karl said.

The headquarters was crowded with thirty or so people manning phones. Knox was behind his desk when Karl led Rollie into the office.

"What do you want, Finch?" Knox said.

"Not much," Rollie said. "Just to see you behind bars for the next twenty-five to life."

Behind Rollie, Karl laughed.

Knox glared at Rollie. "The letter," he said.

Rollie reached into his jacket pocket and set the letter on Knox's desk. "Enjoy," he said.

"Goodbye, Mr. Finch," Knox said.

Rollie turned and walked past Karl, opened the door, and let himself out.

Walking toward 47th Street, Rollie felt Karl following him again. At the parking garage, Rollie took the elevator up to the 5th level, even though his car was parked on level three.

He stood beside the closed elevator door and waited. He could hear the elevator in motion. When it stopped and the door opened, Karl stepped out and Rollie tripped him with his foot and then rushed into the elevator and rode down to level one.

Rollie ran into the coffee shop across the street, ordered a coffee, and went over to wait by the window.

After a few minutes, Karl emerged from the garage and headed back toward 51st Street.

"And so it goes," Rollie said as he sipped coffee.

•　　•　　•

After dropping off a dozen donuts to the detectives, Rollie took Teal to lunch at the diner a few blocks from the precinct.

"To what do I owe this free lunch?" Teal said as he bit into a bacon cheeseburger.

Rollie handed Teal a copy of Pearly's letter.

"Don't get any grease on it," Rollie said.

Teal read the letter as he ate. "Jesus Christ, Rollie," he said.

"We don't need Jesus, we need the commissioner," Rollie said.

"I just waltz into his office and say, 'here, read this'?" Teal said.

"That's exactly what you do," Rollie said.

"And what do I do after I'm fired?" Teal said.

"I gave a copy to Knox this morning," Rollie said.

"What the fuck for?" Teal said.

"If he takes this seriously, he'll make some calls to his lawyers, who will, in turn, make some calls to the commissioner," Rollie said.

"Who will, in turn, call me and ream me a new one," Teal said.

"Not if you convince the commissioner that Knox will call only if he feels threatened. And why else would he feel threatened besides his own guilt?" Rollie said.

Teal stared at Rollie for a moment. "You're paying for dessert, too."

"Let's take a ride tomorrow."

"When do you want me to talk to the commissioner?"

"After he calls you," Rollie said. "That way we know Knox is worried."

"Rollie, you ever think about coming back," Teal said, "I can have you reinstated. The force needs detectives like you."

"My daughters need me," Rollie said. "I'll pick you up at 8:00."

.   .   .

Back at his desk, Rollie called Joanna. She was still in Florida, but leaving in a few days to get ready for the new school year.

"I have a few things to cover with you," Rollie said. "I spoke to Al Timmons in person. He remembers the case vividly and believes that Knox is guilty. He was ordered to drop the case because it was felt at the time that the city couldn't afford a scandal like that so soon after the Trade Center."

"Felt by whom?" Joanna said.

"By people who are no longer in charge," Rollie said. "One of whom wrote a letter asking the case to be reopened."

"Will they take him seriously?" Joanna said.

"We'll know soon enough," Rollie said. "I gave Knox a copy of the letter. If he calls the police commissioner to complain, we'll know Knox is concerned."

"Was he?" Joanna said. "Concerned, I mean."

"Enough so that he had me followed," Rollie said.

"Who followed you?" Joanna said.

"Some goon who works for him," Rollie said. "The point is, Knox is concerned enough to put a tail on me."

"I didn't think anybody could get to that cold-hearted son of a bitch," Joanna said.

"There's something else, too," Rollie said. "I located Knox's cabin in the Catskills. He sold it in 2007 after his father died. It's on a small lake and surrounded by thick woods. I think Julia's buried there, and that Knox got the speeding ticket hurrying back to Manhattan."

"Captain Teal was right when he said you were a great detective, Rollie," Joanna said. "But please be careful. Knox is a dangerous man."

"Don't worry, and I'll call you soon with an update," Rollie said.

After hanging up with Joanna, Rollie went to the kitchen for a cup of coffee and found the girls going through Georgia's cookbook once again.

"What are you looking for?" Rollie said.

"That recipe for lamb chops," Grace said.

"Found it," Giselle said.

"I'll be back in a bit to help you girls," Rollie said.

He returned to his office and started whittling down the large stack of mail on his desk. There were two large checks from law firms he had done work for just before Joanna Kearns showed up.

Stuck in the middle of the pack was a thank you card from Joanna with another check for five thousand tucked inside. She wrote that she knows he had been underpaid and hoped he would continue on.

Once the mail was manageable, Rollie returned to the kitchen to help the girls with dinner.

"Mom has two lamb chop recipes," Grace said. "One for the oven and one for the grill."

"The grill is better," Rollie said. "I'll handle that and you guys do the rest."

Rollie went to the backyard to heat up the grill. Ten minutes later, Grace carried a tray with three pounds of lamb chops on it and set it on the small shelf attached to the grill.

"We're doing mashed potatoes, corn, and carrots," Grace said.

"The chops will take fifteen minutes," Rollie said.

"Everything else will be ready," Grace said.

Rollie gave the chops seven minutes per side, and used the time to think and work out his notes in his mind.

Knox killed her, of that he had no doubt.

Strangulation was most likely. No screams and no blood to clean up. Julia Knox was a small woman. He could easily fold her into a contractor bag and store her someplace safe.

Where?

He didn't dispose of the body for one week. Timmons had searched the apartment and found nothing out of place. A good detective like Timmons would not have missed a body hidden in the bathtub.

What he did was….

Rollie flipped the lamb chops.

What he did was, while the world watched the horror of 9/11 unfold, he waited for night to come, then retrieved his car from the garage on 103rd Street, drove it to the apartment, and put the body in the trunk.

A week later he drove to his cabin in the Catskills to bury her.

Rollie's theory fit like a glove.

He carried the lamb chops to the dinner table and said, "Let's go out for ice cream for dessert."

CHAPTER TWENTY-ONE

Teal chomped on two chocolate donuts as Rollie drove north on the New York Thruway to the Catskills.

"How am I supposed to buy you lunch after those two donuts?" Rollie said.

"You'll find a way," Teal said.

Rollie had picked up donuts and coffee before heading out, and Teal had eaten two of them before 9:00 in the morning.

"Anything from the commissioner yet?" Rollie said.

"I would have mentioned it," Teal said.

"His lawyers will call," Rollie said. "Bet on it."

"Anymore donuts?" Teal said.

"Just the one I bought for me," Rollie said.

Teal grabbed the bag, opened it, and removed the cream donut and said, "I love these."

"Help yourself," Rollie said.

Teal bit into the donut and licked cream off his fingers. "Good," he said.

"Your wife would kill me if she knew I was encouraging you to eat like this," Rollie said.

"Tonight when I get home, dinner will be Swiss chard soup, followed by a leafy green salad with no-fat dressing," Teal said. "Dessert will be a Weight Watchers cookie the size of a quarter."

"What's that taste like?" Rollie said.

"Not like a cream donut," Teal said.

"So, listen to my theory," Rollie said. "On the morning of 9/11, Knox murders his wife by strangulation so there won't be any blood to clean up. Once his rage calms down and he realizes what he's done, the terrorists give him the perfect cover story. She died in Tower One. However, he still needs to get rid of the body, so what does he do?"

Teal ate the last bit of donut and licked his fingers. "You tell me," he said.

"He goes shopping for large contractor bags and stuffs her into a bag, and then waits for night. Which explains why he didn't answer the phone until 11:30 in the morning, he was out bag shopping. Late at night, he retrieves his car from the garage on 103rd Street, drives to the apartment and takes the body down using the service elevator, goes out through the alleyway and drives back to the garage. Where the body sits in the trunk until he drives to his cabin in the Catskills."

Sipping coffee, Teal nodded. "When Timmons shows up to look around, there's nothing to see," he said.

"It fits," Rollie said.

"Like a glove," Teal said. "How do we prove it?"

"Do you know how many murderers we've put away without a body?" Rollie said.

"Yes, with strong circumstantial evidence," Teal said. "Not with a twenty-year-old phone bill."

An hour later, Rollie parked on the side of the dirt road at Big Pond Lake.

"That's the cabin down there," Rollie said.

They walked down to the cabin and Teal said, "It's not a cabin anymore. Someone put some money into this place."

"Twenty years ago, at night, Knox carried his wife's body into the woods and buried her," Rollie said. "Let's take a walk."

They returned to the road and entered the woods.

The tall pine trees created deep shade, and twenty yards in, the woods were fairly dark.

"She was a small woman, around a hundred and fifteen pounds," Rollie said. "But carrying her and a lantern and a shovel, she's going to get heavy. How far does he go before he buries her? A hundred feet? Two hundred? The grave can't be too far in."

"And covered with twenty years of growth," Teal said. "It's a needle in a haystack, Rollie. At best."

"But not impossible," Rollie said.

"All you need to do is find a judge willing to grant a warrant to tear up miles of pristine woods looking for a woman that the rest of the world thinks was killed on 9/11," Teal said. "Know any?"

"Let's go to lunch," Rollie said.

"Good. I'm getting bit," Teal said.

•   •   •

At the diner in Andes, Rollie nodded to the photograph on the wall and said, "See anybody you know?"

Biting into a bacon cheeseburger, Teal looked at the photograph. "Knox and his father, so what?" he said.

"So, being able to prove he once owned that cabin and fished in the local tournaments makes it impossible for Knox to deny he knows the region," Rollie said.

"Yeah, but who's asking?" Teal said.

"I am," Rollie said.

"What do they got for dessert here?" Teal said.

• • •

Rollie was sipping coffee from a chair opposite Teal's desk.

Behind his desk, Teal said, "Besides mosquito bites, what do we got that we could use for a warrant?"

"What we could use is a friendly judge that hates Knox," Rollie said.

"Hold that thought," Teal said as his phone rang.

Teal answered, listened for a moment, and then said, "Yes sir," and hung up.

He looked at Rollie. "That was Commissioner Andrews," he said. "He wants us in his office at 11:00 tomorrow morning."

"Us?" Rollie said. "I'm not on the job anymore."

"If you value your pension, benefits, and P.I. license, you'll show up at eleven o'clock tomorrow morning," Teal said.

"Should I bring the donuts?" Rollie said.

"What you should bring are body bags, one for each of us," Teal said.

CHAPTER TWENTY-TWO

Before dinner, Rollie sat at his desk and pulled up a map online of the Big Pond area and surrounding woodlands.

The woods were deep, maybe a dozen square miles before the next road.

How far would Knox carry the body of his wife before enough was enough? Fifty yards? A hundred yards? More?

Picking up a hundred-and-fifteen-pound woman is one thing, carrying her dead-weight body a long distance was something else. And, of course, a shovel and lantern.

One hundred yards was Rollie's guess.

Teal was right in that twenty years of growth would make the grave nearly impossible to locate.

Rollie picked up the original copy of the letter Timmons wrote. Knox's lawyers must have given the mayor and commissioner an earful by now.

Despite his bravado, Knox was worried. Even a hint of a scandal at this point could cost him the election and he knew it.

The question in Rollie's mind was: how far was Knox willing to go?

Grace stepped into the office. "Dad, dinner," she said.

•   •   •

"When does school start up again?" Rollie asked at the dinner table.

"Five weeks," Grace said. "Right after Labor Day."

Giselle looked at Grace and nodded.

"What?" Rollie said.

"Nothing," Grace said.

"Oh, tell him," Gloria said.

"Nobody asked you," Grace said.

"Tell me what?" Rollie said.

"The high school has a welcome back dance a week before school starts," Giselle said.

"And what's the problem?" Rollie said.

"You mean, I can go?" Grace said.

"Of course you can go," Rollie said.

"I need a gown and shoes," Grace said. "And a handbag."

"Go get them," Rollie said. "I have to work tomorrow, but the next day we'll go to the mall."

"We'll help," Giselle said.

"Something age-appropriate," Rollie said.

"I told you he'd say that," Gloria said.

"Never you mind, or you'll spend the next five weeks grounded," Rollie said.

"Consider me silent," Gloria said.

"Good. Can you silently pass the potatoes?" Rollie said.

•   •   •

Rollie was up at 6:30, showered, changed and made breakfast for the girls before eight o'clock.

He left at 8:30 and arrived at the Midtown Precinct at 9:45.

Teal was waiting for him in the parking lot.

"We'll take my car," Teal said.

"But the body bags are in my trunk," Rollie said.

"Never mind the body bags, just get in," Teal said.

The drive to One Police Plaza near City Hall was not quite five miles away, but it might as well have been fifty, traffic was so congested.

"I feel like I've been called to the principal's office," Teal said.

"I'll buy lunch," Rollie said.

"Fucking right, you'll buy lunch," Teal said.

At 10:45, Teal parked in the reserved lot for police personnel.

"Should I get some donuts?" Rollie said.

"What you should do is shut up," Teal said.

"Relax, Bill, he's just going to ask a few questions," Rollie said.

They entered the building, went through screening, and took the elevator to Commissioner Andrews's office.

A civilian receptionist ushered them into the large and impressive office, where Andrews sat behind am equally impressive redwood desk.

Andrews stood and nodded to the receptionist, and she closed the door on her way out.

"To the conference table," Andrews said.

Rollie and Teal followed Andrews to the table where a silver platter of donuts and bagels and a pot of coffee were arranged.

Andrews filled three cups and took a seat beside a thick file folder. "Please be seated," he said.

Rollie and Teal took chairs.

"I received a visit from an attorney representing John Knox, front runner for New York governor," Andrews said. "Needless to say, he wasn't too happy. Do you want to know why?"

"He received the letter I delivered to John Knox," Rollie said.

Andrews looked at Rollie. "I pulled your file, Mr. Finch," he said. "You were an excellent police officer and an outstanding detective.

You retired early, after your wife died, to raise your three daughters. That makes you an outstanding father in my book."

"Thank you," Rollie said.

"Please explain to me why you believe that Knox is guilty of murdering his wife," Andrews said. "I know what I read in the letter, but I'd like to hear it from you."

Rollie began with Joanna Kearns, the phone call, the subway ride to Chambers Street, then the cabin on Big Pond, the speeding ticket, Timmons's report, the service elevator at the apartment, and ended with, "I looked into his eyes."

Andrews listened carefully, and when Rollie had finished, he looked at Teal. "You were partners once, is that why you're involved in this?" he said.

"My doing, Commissioner," Rollie said. "I needed a contact still on the job who could open a few doors for me."

Andrews sighed as he opened the file next to him and removed the letter. "John Knox, in all likelihood, will be our next governor," he said. "I've discussed this with departmental attorneys and the district attorney, and the opinion is they wouldn't touch it with a ten-foot pole. Captain Teal, you are to discontinue any activity into John Knox. Is that clear?"

"Yes, Commissioner," Teal said.

Andrews looked at Rollie.

"Mr. Finch, if I had your license revoked, would you still continue your investigation?" Andrews said.

"Yes, I would," Rollie said. "As a private citizen."

"Exactly what I thought," Andrews said. "On the record, there will be not additional police activity concerning John Knox. Is that clear, Captain Teal?"

"Very," Teal said.

"Mr. Finch, when you continue your investigation, you are to advise Captain Teal of all your progress until such time as there is enough evidence for the department to officially proceed," Andrews said. "Off the record, of course. Is that understood, Mr. Finch?"

"Yes," Rollie said.

Rollie and Teal looked at Andrews.

"I don't like John Knox," Andrews said. "That's all, gentlemen."

Rollie and Teal stood.

"Captain, wait outside for a moment," Andrews said.

Teal left the office.

"Mr. Finch, however this goes, when this is over, give some consideration to returning to the department," Andrews said. "This city needs cops like you, and there is an opening for Assistant Chief of Detectives."

Rollie nodded. "I will give it some thought," he said.

·   ·   ·

As he sliced into a thick steak, Teal said, "I always wanted to eat at Delmonico's."

"What's your wife going to say?" Rollie said.

"Nothing, because I'm not going to tell her," Teal said. "Tonight, when she serves me carrot sticks and lettuce leaves, I'm going to remember this thick hunk of beef and smile."

"Andrews offered me a position," Rollie said.

"Of course he did," Teal said. "And you said?"

"I told him I'll think about it," Rollie said.

Teal held up a forkful of beef and said, "Oh baby."

"How do you want to handle Knox?" Rollie said.

"You heard the commissioner," Teal said. "You do all the work and I get all the credit."

"That's what I thought he said," Rollie said as he chewed on a piece of his steak.

· · ·

At his desk, Rollie called Joanna Kearns. She had flown back to South Carolina.

He carefully explained to her the latest developments.

"It sounds like he's worried," Joanna said.

"Maybe not about being arrested, but a scandal would cost him the election and he knows it," Rollie said.

"It's much more than I hoped for," Joanna said. "Maybe preventing him from becoming governor is enough."

"I won't give up until he's behind bars," Rollie said.

CHAPTER TWENTY-THREE

As promised, Rollie drove the girls to the mall in Valley Stream to shop for Grace's gown to wear to the welcome back dance.

The mall opened at 10:00. They waited with a hundred others for the doors to open, and then they walked to the store that specialized in gowns.

While Grace, Giselle, and Gloria shopped, Rollie strolled over to an electronics store and browsed gadgets. He wound up buying a pen that wrote upside down and a small flashlight that made the claim it could withstand being run over by a tank. He didn't believe the claim, but he needed a flashlight for the glove box.

When Rollie returned to the girls, they had narrowed the search to six gowns.

Grace tried on each gown for Rollie until she eliminated four.

"It's between these two," she said.

"From experience, I know what your mother would advise," Rollie said.

The girls looked at him.

"Your mother always picked out a pair of shoes she liked best first, and then matched the dress to them," Rollie said.

Grace turned to the sales woman.

"Follow me," the woman said.

While the girls went shoe shopping, Rollie went to an athletic apparel store and picked up some new gym clothes.

He returned to the gowns store to find Grace wearing two different shoes.

"I can't decide," Grace said.

"Try on the gowns with both shoes and pick what you like best," Rollie said.

Grace tried on one gown and then the other. "I love them both," she said.

"When is your birthday?" Rollie said.

"Three weeks," Grace said.

"I'd like to be out of this store by then," Rollie said.

"I can't decide," Grace said.

"Take them both," Rollie said. "Wear one to the welcome back dance, and the other to your senior prom at the end of the year."

"Really?" Grace said.

"If it gets us out of this store, yes, really," Rollie said.

"What do we get?" Gloria said.

"Lunch," Rollie said.

After paying for the gowns, shoes, and handbag, Rollie took the girls to a family-style restaurant near the mall.

By the time they returned home, it was 3:00 in the afternoon. Rollie changed into his new sweats and knocked out an hour on the step climber.

He let his thoughts wander. Was Joanna correct that keeping Knox out of the governor's chair enough?

To Rollie, that was like arresting Al Capone, a mass murderer and gangster, for not paying his taxes.

The punishment didn't fit the crime, but it had dethroned Capon as the kingpin of gangsters.

Knox murdered his wife. That's what he should go down for.

His punishment shouldn't be just losing an election.

Almost three thousand people died when the Towers were attacked, but Julia Knox wasn't one of them.

She was…

"Dad, we're low on groceries," Grace said as she entered the office.

"Make a list, take two hundred dollars from my wallet and the car keys, and drive your sisters to the store," Rollie said.

"So, I'm fully out of the doghouse?" Grace said.

"Don't let it go to your head," Rollie said. "And Grace…"

"I know, I know," Grace said. "Responsibility."

After Grace left, Rollie finished the hour on the step climber and then took a shower. He tossed on clean sweats, made some coffee, and went to his desk.

On a whim, he called Knox's headquarters in Manhattan. Knox had returned to Albany. Rollie went to Knox's election campaign website. Knox was stumping throughout the state.

Albany, Buffalo, Troy, Syracuse, and Manhattan, all within one week.

Rollie called Joanna at her home in South Carolina.

"Hello, Rollie," she said.

"Hi, Joanna," Rollie said. "I was wondering if you felt like a bit of fun."

"Fun?"

"At Knox's expense," Rollie said.

"What kind of fun?" Joanna said.

"Knox is stumping with fundraisers," Rollie said. "Two-hundred-and-fifty-dollar-a-plate dinners. How would you like to be my date for the Manhattan fundraiser at the Hilton Ballroom?"

"Are you serious?" Joanna said.

"I am. The price of the ticket would be worth it just to see Knox's face when he sees us sitting at a table," Rollie said.

"When?" Joanna said.

"Next Thursday night," Rollie said.

"Alright, it's a date," Joanna said. "It's only a seven-hour drive; I think I'll drive it rather than fly."

"And forget about a hotel, you'll stay with us," Rollie said.

"I couldn't."

"You could."

"Alright, Rollie, I'll stay with you," Joanna said. "I'll be there Wednesday afternoon."

"It's formal," Rollie said.

"No worries."

After hanging up with Joanna, Rollie called Teal at his office.

"Knox is having a fundraiser at the Hilton next Thursday night," Rollie said.

"Bully for Knox," Teal said.

"I'm attending and accompanying Joanna Kearns as her escort," Rollie said.

"Jesus, Rollie. Why?" Teal said.

"Rattle his cage, see how well he holds up," Rollie said.

"I'd go but I don't want to," Teal said. "Besides, it's up to the department who they endorse."

"I know that," Rollie said. "That's not why I called. I'd like you to come to dinner Wednesday night so we can chat with Joanna Kearns. She'll be staying over."

"With you?"

"And the girls," Rollie said.

"What's on the menu?"

"As long as it's not lettuce and carrot sticks, does it matter?" Rollie said.

"What time?"

. . .

At dinner, Rollie said, "How did you do shopping?"

"Got everything on our list, and brought back eight dollars in change," Grace said.

"I want you to go through your mother's cookbook and find something special for dinner next Wednesday night," Rollie said.

"What's Wednesday?" Grace said.

"A day of the week, stupid," Gloria said.

"You walked into that one," Giselle said.

"The both of you are going to walk straight into the doghouse," Grace said.

"So what happens next Wednesday?" Giselle said.

"Joanna Kearns, as part of this case I'm working on, is coming for a visit," Rollie said. "She'll be here Wednesday, as will your Uncle Bill. So, dinner is in your hands."

"What should we make?" Grace said.

"As long as there are no lettuce leaves, kale, or raw carrots, it's up to you," Rollie said.

"What's kale?" Gloria said.

"Wait, is she staying over?" Grace said.

"Probably until Friday morning," Rollie said.

"I can double up with Giselle," Grace said.

"No you can't," Giselle said. "You snore."

"I don't snore," Grace said.

"Relax, girls. I have a perfectly fine daybed in my office," Rollie said.

Grace looked at Giselle and Gloria. "So, what should we make?"

"No raw carrots or kale, whatever that is," Giselle said.

"Or lettuce leaves," Gloria said.

CHAPTER TWENTY-FOUR

After breakfast, Rollie called Teal at his office.

"I ordered two tickets to Knox's event at the Hilton. Sure you don't want to go?" Rollie said.

"I'm good with that one, buddy," Teal said. "But maybe I should hang around the lobby, in case there is trouble."

"Knox is too smart to pull anything in public," Rollie said. "But there is something you can do for me."

"And what's that?"

"Knox's right hand man is a big guy. Knox called him Karl. Can you get a bead on him?"

"Karl what?"

"That's all I got, but if he's working for Knox, his name is out there somewhere."

"What's he done?"

"Followed me twice from Knox's headquarters on 51st to the parking garage on 47th," Rollie said.

"I'll run it down."

"Thanks."

"So, what are you making for dinner Wednesday?"

"Me, nothing, but the girls are," Rollie said.

"Good, then I know it will be fattening as hell."

"Call me when you get a lead on this Karl character," Rollie said.

He hung up and went to the kitchen where the girls were rifling thought their mother's cookbook.

"Anything?" he said.

"What does Uncle Walt like?" Grace said.

"Anything as long as it's fattening," Rollie said.

"Swiss chard soup with tiny meatballs?" Grace said.

"Too veggie," Rollie said.

"Veal parmesan with angel hair pasta and homemade garlic bread?" Grace said.

"Excellent."

"What about dessert?" Giselle said.

"Ah, your mom's specialty," Rollie said. "Did you get any heavy cream at the store?"

"No, it wasn't on our list," Grace said.

"Your mom has some mason jars under the sink," Rollie said. "Wash them out and I'll be right back. Gloria, you come with me."

"How come?" Gloria said.

"Somebody has to push the cart," Rollie said.

At the store, Rollie bought two pints of heavy cream, a quart of whipping cream, and a bottle of vanilla.

"Dad, we didn't even need a cart for this," Gloria said.

"I know, but I miss my youngest daughter," Rollie said.

At home, Rollie said, "We going to make very fattening ice cream for dessert tonight, topped with fresh whipped cream."

"What do we do?" Grace said.

"Grab a mason jar," Rollie said. "Pour in one cup of the heavy cream, a pinch of salt, one and a half teaspoons of vanilla, and one and a half teaspoons of sugar."

"How much is a pinch?" Grace said.

"Pick some up with two fingers," Rollie said.

The girls added the ingredients to the mason jar.

"Now what?" Grace said.

"Shake the jar for five minutes and put it in the freezer," Rollie said. "We'll try it tonight."

"That's it?" Grace said.

"That's it," Rollie said.

"What about dinner for tonight?" Grace said.

"Call me when it's ready," Rollie said.

•   •   •

Rollie spent the afternoon on the phone with a prominent law firm in Manhattan that was preparing the defense of a major Broadway actor accused of rape.

They needed background reports on all witnesses for both sides, and requested Rollie read the arrest reports and statements made by all parties.

Rollie was looking at forty to sixty hours of billable work at one-fifty and hour, so he took the assignment.

The law firm emailed documents in PDF format, but there were some classified documents that he had to pick up in person.

He read the initial charges first.

The actor was fifty-two years old and had starred in five consecutive hit Broadway plays spanning a decade. His latest play had been running for more than a year and showed no signs of slowing down. Tickets ranged from five hundred dollars to two thousand a seat.

After twelve months, he took the play to London, then several other major cities in Europe before returning to a dozen cities in America.

Rumors of sexual misconduct had followed the actor for years, but charges had never been filed against him. Until now.

An actress, hired to play in several crowd scenes and as a backup singer, claimed that the actor drugged and raped her in their hotel in London.

The actor denied all charges.

The alleged rape took place nearly nine months earlier, and the publicity had increased ticket sales to the point that the play could run for another year.

Provided the lead actor wasn't in prison, of course.

The plus side for the actor was there was zero evidence to back up the claim.

The negative side for the actor was that he now had the reputation of a total womanizer.

The witness list was long, including witnesses in London.

Rollie started on the witness statements and lost himself in time until Grace popped in and announced dinner.

The girls had made broiled lemon/pepper chicken with mashed potatoes and corn, using their mother's recipe for the chicken.

The girls were becoming quite adept in the kitchen.

After dinner, they whipped up enough fresh whipped cream for the mason jar of ice cream, and they all tried a bowl for dessert.

"Uncle Bill is going to love this," Gloria said as she ate a spoonful.

CHAPTER TWENTY-FIVE

First thing in the morning, Rollie drove to the posh law offices of Gitter and Kline on Park Avenue South and 31st Street.

The actor was a millionaire many times over, so he could afford the lavish fees of Gitter and Kline.

The address was lavish, the offices were lavish, and so were their suits.

Rollie had been hired by them at least six times in the past.

Gitter and Kline, men in their sixties with perfect haircuts and tailored suits, met Rollie in one of their conference rooms.

"Our goal is a dismissal at the trial in three months," Gitter said. "And with your help, Rollie, we'll get it."

"If they bring a guilty verdict in London, the trial in America will be delayed for years with appeals, and no one wants that," Kline said.

"The witness list in London, I'd like to tackle that first," Rollie said. "If the witnesses are weak, we could probably get a walk at home."

"Very good, Rollie," Kline said. "When do you want to go?"

"Next week sometime," Rollie said. "I'll let you know in a few days. One thing, I have to bring my girls. I'll pay their expenses myself."

"Get a dismissal and we'll gladly include them in your expenses," Gitter said. "Our Broadway star can afford it."

"I'll call you Wednesday," Rollie said.

"You'll need this," Kline said and handed Rollie a folder.

•   •   •

"Don't you ever get sick of this place?" Rollie said, treating Teal to another lunch at the diner near the precinct.

"Last night, I had spinach soup with no seasoning, a lettuce and cucumber salad with pepper, no dressing, and a cookie so small a single ant could have carried it away," Teal said.

"When is your physical?" Rollie said.

"Five weeks," Teal said.

"I brought you this," Rollie said and placed a small drugstore bag on the table.

"What is it?" Teal said.

"Two tablets with every meal reduces cholesterol," Rollie said.

Teal removed the bottle from the bag. "Thanks, Rollie."

"About Karl?" Rollie said.

Teal pulled an envelope from his pocket and handed it to Rollie.

"Karl is Karl Clapper," Teal said.

"Like the clap on, clap off Clapper?" Rollie said.

"Spelled the same," Teal said. "He was a cop for twelve years. Had sixteen formal complaints for excessive force before the department said enough was enough. How he hooked up with Knox is anybody's guess. He's a dangerous one, this guy."

Rollie pocketed the envelope. "Want dessert?"

"Hell, yes," Teal said and opened the bottle of pills.

•   •   •

When Rollie got home, he called a family meeting in the living room.

"What did we do wrong?" Grace said.

"Who said you did anything wrong?" Rollie said.

"Family meeting…" Giselle said.

"…means we did something wrong," Gloria said.

"Not this time," Rollie said.

"Then what?" Grace said.

"Tomorrow morning, we have to go to the post office and get you passports with a rush order," Rollie said.

"Why?" Grace said.

"Because I have to go to London on business, and I can't leave you home alone," Rollie said.

"Wait, what? We're going to London?" Grace said.

"We need clothes," Giselle said.

"What do they wear in London?" Gloria said. "Like, big hats with feathers and gloves and stuff?"

"How long will we be there?" Giselle said.

"Five days."

"We need to get ready," Grace said. "We need new clothes and…"

"What you have is fine," Rollie said. "They dress just like you."

"Are you sure?" Giselle said.

"London is on the other side of the world, isn't it winter there right now?" Gloria said.

"It's summer like here; they're in the Northern Hemisphere just like us." Rollie said. "Now, tomorrow we get you passports."

"We have to look up stuff to do there," Grace said. "Come on, girls."

While the girls went to Grace's room, Rollie made some fresh coffee and took a cup to his office.

Karl Clapper was a rough customer, according to the report Teal gave him. Twelve years on the job, three shootings, and sixteen complaints for use of excessive force against suspects.

He liked the 110 Precinct so he could work the Harlem streets. His final straw came when he beat a suspect into a coma in a back alleyway on 123rd Street.

There was a long gap between the time he was terminated from the department until he hooked up with Knox and became his personal driver about six years ago.

Rollie read the sixteen complaints against Karl. Each was worse than the one before it. The three shootings he was involved in resulted in two deaths. Of the sixteen incidents of excessive force, three resulted in deaths.

As a cop, he had killed five people. Who knows what he's done since?

Why did Knox hire a man like this as his driver?

The only logical answer was muscle.

•   •   •

At the dinner table, the girls talked more than they ate. Their excitement level over London was through the roof.

"Dad, are you going to do any sightseeing with us?" Grace said.

"Maybe a little, we'll see," Rollie said. "But there is one thing you need to promise me: the three of you will never lose sight of each other. London is like any other big city and it can be dangerous, so you three will have to look out for each other the whole time."

"We promise," Grace said.

"After dinner, show me your plans," Rollie said.

CHAPTER TWENTY-SIX

As Rollie drove home on Queens Boulevard, the girls compared their passport photos.

"I look like a complete nerd," Grace said.

"You look fine," Rollie said.

"Why aren't I smiling?" Giselle said. "I should have smiled."

"You also look fine," Rollie said.

"Why do I look like an orphan?" Gloria said.

Rollie turned down their street.

"I didn't get an 'I look fine'," Gloria said.

"It's implied," Rollie said.

• • •

While the girls made dinner, Rollie called Joanna.

"What time can we expect you?" Rollie said.

"I plan to leave at 7:00, so right around 3:00 in the afternoon," Joanna said.

"Excellent. Plenty of time to rest up for dinner," Rollie said.

"Rollie, what do you think Knox will do when he sees us in the audience?"

"He may not show it, but he'll be rattled. The real reaction will come later in the form of more phone calls."

"Rollie, are we doing the right thing?" Joanna said.

"We are if you want to stop a murderer from becoming the next governor of New York," Rollie said.

"I'll see you tomorrow," Joanna said.

After hanging up with Joanna, Rollie called Teal at his office. "Not that I need to remind you about dinner, but tomorrow at 6:30."

"I'll be there with bells on," Teal said.

"Leave the bells home and bring your appetite," Rollie said.

After Teal, Rollie called Gitter and Kline.

"I'll be flying to London next Saturday and taking depositions starting Monday," Rollie said. "If you could call the inspectors handling the case and let them know I'm coming, that would be a big help."

"I'll call them right now and arrange for a deposition room," Kline said.

"Thanks," Rollie said. "Call me with the contact names when you have them."

"Will do, Rollie," Kline said.

After signing off with Kline, Rollie changed into sweats and did an hour on the step climber.

Joanna's question was on his mind. What would Knox do when he saw them at a table? That was what he wanted to find out.

Would Knox fold his hand?

Would he grow enraged and take action?

What would he do?

•　　•　　•

At the dinner table, Rollie said, "Our flight is booked for 7:00 a.m. this Saturday. Make sure you're packed and ready to go Friday night."

"Why so early?" Grace said.

"You won't think it's so early when we land," Rollie said. "It's an eight hour flight, and the time difference is five hours. So when we land, back here it's five o'clock, but there it's 10:00 at night."

"What do we wear on the plane?" Grace said.

"Something comfortable, it's a long flight," Rollie said. "Jeans and sneakers will do nicely."

"On Sunday, do you have to work?" Giselle said.

"No, but I do need to check in with the police inspector," Rollie said. "That shouldn't take more than an hour, so we'll have plenty of time to sightsee."

"And eat," Gloria said. "I've been reading about the food and they eat buttered bacon sandwiches."

"That sounds gross," Giselle said.

"Reserve judgment until you try it," Rollie said. "Now tomorrow, do you want help with dinner?"

"We got it covered, Dad," Grace said.

•   •   •

After dinner, Rollie returned to his office for a while. He reread the reports given to him by Gitter and Kline again.

On the surface they were damaging.

What was below the surface?

There are facts, and then there are *facts*.

Rollie knew from years of police work that most people believed their opinions constituted fact.

That was the surface.

The police detective's job was to go below the surface for the real truth.

And that was the reason why Rollie was going to London to take depositions from witnesses, to learn the truth.

CHAPTER TWENTY-SEVEN

The girls answered the door when Joanna knocked. They greeted her with hugs and kisses, and the greeting was returned in kind.

Rollie came in from his office in time to rescue Joanna.

"Girls, she just drove seven hours to get here," Rollie said. "Show her to my room and give her a chance to freshen up a bit before you smother her."

A little later, while the girls played soccer in the backyard, Rollie and Joanna sat in the shade at the patio table with glasses of ginger ale.

"I've noticed that you never drink alcohol," Joanna said.

"I'm raising girls, not saints," Rollie said. "Temptation isn't there if it doesn't exist."

"Are you speaking from experience?" Joanna said.

"When I was sixteen, my friends convinced me to raid my parent's liquor cabinet," Rollie said. "We drank an entire bottle of brandy. I was sick for days."

"What did your parents do?" Joanna said.

"Nothing. They thought I'd been punished enough by the hangover," Rollie said. "However, they did put a lock on the liquor cabinet."

The girls broke up the game and headed to the kitchen. "We have to start dinner," Grace said.

Once the girls were inside, Joanna said, "Rollie, have you ever thought, what would happen to the girls if something happened to you?"

"Of course, but it's not going to come from the likes of John Knox," Rollie said.

"How can you be so sure?" Joanna said.

"He doesn't want to mess up his perfect hair," Rollie said.

Joanna grinned. "Should I help the girls with dinner?"

"You can help by eating," Rollie said.

"The girls said Captain Teal was also coming," Joanna said.

"He's been a big help with Knox," Rollie said.

"I think I might want to take a shower and change before dinner. Do you mind?" Joanna said.

"Not at all," Rollie said.

•   •   •

"This veal is incredible," Teal said.

"Our mom's recipe," Grace said.

"And we made dessert, so save room," Giselle said.

"You bet," Teal added.

After dinner and before dessert, the girls cleaned up the kitchen, and Rollie, Teal, and Joanna took coffee to the backyard patio table.

"Doors open at 7:00," Rollie said. "Dinner is 7:30 to 8:30. Knox gets introduced during dessert and is expected to speak for one hour. He won't be having dinner, I guess to make a bigger entrance."

"I think I should be there, just in case," Teal said.

"Knox is way too smart to pull anything in public," Rollie said. "Besides, I plan for us to walk out on him after he sees us."

"I'm going to hang around anyway," Teal said. "That is, if you don't mind."

"Up to you, but it will be a waste of time," Rollie said.

Grace came out to the yard. "Dessert," she announced

Rollie, Joanna, and Teal followed Grace to the dining room where six bowls were arranged on the table. Grace served the ice cream topped with whipped cream and chocolate syrup, while Giselle and Gloria served Rollie, Joanna, and Teal fresh coffee.

"Girls, I am a happy man," Teal said.

· · ·

Before leaving, Teal and Rollie went to Rollie's office.

"This Clapper is a piece of work," Teal said. "I'd like to keep an eye on him tomorrow night."

"Can you do it without being seen?" Rollie said. "I don't want to tip our hand."

"What exactly is your hand, if I may ask?" Teal said.

"Rattle the cage and see what falls out until I can put together enough evidence to bring to you for a warrant," Rollie said. "After which, I bow out and let you take all the credit for my hard work."

"And don't think I won't," Teal said. "But right now I have to get home or my wife is going to think I'm having an affair."

After Teal left, Rollie sat at the backyard patio table and sipped ginger ale from the can.

He heard the kitchen door slide open, and Joanna joined him.

"This has been a lovely evening, Rollie," she said. "Thank you."

"It was mostly the girls' doing," Rollie said. "Where are they? It's pretty quiet in there."

"They went to Grace's room to look online at things to do in London," Joanna said.

"Again?" Rollie said.

"Rollie, I know it's none of my business, but why are you going to London?" Joanna asked.

"For a law firm," Rollie said. "To take depositions for a pending trial. I'll be gone five days."

"I think it's really special that you'd take your girls rather than hire a house sitter," Joanna said.

"I consider it part of their education," Rollie said.

Joanna nodded. "Well, we have a big night tomorrow," she said. "And thank you for the use of your room."

"Goodnight," Rollie said.

A little while later, Rollie went to his office where he had set up the daybed earlier. The bed had a decent mattress and pillow, and he fell asleep almost immediately.

He woke up around 3:00 in the morning, turned on the light, and went to his desk. He made a note to himself to check the World Trade Center recovery website at some point and then returned to bed.

It was amazing how many personal items belonging to victims had been recovered in the twenty years since the Towers came down.

Personal items such as wedding rings and jewelry were used to help identify victims with a fair measure of success.

It wasn't much, just a loose thread to tie up.

Thinking about that, Rollie fell back asleep.

CHAPTER TWENTY-EIGHT

In the morning, Rollie took the girls and Joanna to the family diner on Queens Boulevard for breakfast.

They ordered buttermilk pancakes with sausage, orange juice, and coffee for Rollie and Joanna.

"Dad, can we play soccer in the park for a while?" Grace said.

"I don't see why not," Rollie said.

"I played on my high school and college teams," Joanna said.

"Can she, Dad?" Grace said.

"Don't ask me, ask her," Rollie said.

"Joanna?" Grace said.

"I'll need to change," Joanna said.

"Us, too," Grace said.

After a trip back to the house to change, Rollie drove to the park where the girls and Joanna played a game of shoot-out.

The girls were good, but Joanna taught them a thing or two about the game, surprising everyone as a ringer.

Meanwhile, Rollie thought about Knox and how he would react. Rollie was hoping for anger. Anger was a valuable tool in police work. When a suspect thinks their story is no longer believable, they turn to anger.

The madder Knox got, the guiltier he appeared.

The girls and Joanna played through lunch until around three o'clock. They were hot and sweaty, and Rollie took them to the Dugout for ice cream.

Home by 4:00, Joanna needed to get ready for the evening.

By five o'clock, Rollie was shaved, showered, and dressed in his best black suit. He waited for Joanna in the living room with the girls.

Joanna made her appearance at twenty minutes past five. She wore a black evening dress, sleeveless with a matching shawl. Three-inch heels put her at about five-foot-ten-inches tall. Her hair was worn up, her makeup was flawless, and the girls were blown away.

"She's beautiful," Gloria said.

"Grace, you're in charge until we return; you know the routine," Rollie said.

The ride to Manhattan took an hour. By the time Rollie valet parked the car and they entered the lobby, it was close to seven o'clock.

"I'm very nervous," Joanna said as they walked to the grand ballroom of the hotel.

"Just relax and enjoy the dinner," Rollie said.

"There are a lot of people here," Joanna said.

"One hundred tables with ten to a table," Rollie said. "Knox is doing quite well with his fundraising."

"Everybody is going in," Joanna said. "Do you see Captain Teal anywhere?"

"You won't see Bill unless he wants you to," Rollie said. "Shall we go in?"

Rollie took Joanna's arm and escorted her into the grand ballroom to their table. They had a bird's-eye view of the podium where Knox would stand.

The thousand-strong crowd buzzed with excitement at the prospect of hearing John Knox speak.

Dozens of waiters served dinner, which was salad, roast beef, potatoes and vegetables, and dessert.

Joanna did her best to eat, but her nerves were on edge and the most she could do was pick.

While dessert was being served, the lights over the tables dimmed and a member of Knox's staff went to the illuminated podium.

The excitement reached a fever pitch as he introduced Knox.

Knox walked out waving his hands to a standing ovation. Once he quieted and seated the crowd, Knox worked his magic. For forty-five minutes, he thrilled them with talk of new government mixed in with personal stories.

Around 9:15, Knox announced the "questions and answers" part of the festivities.

The lights over the tables came on, and Knox smiled at his adoring audience.

Until he spotted Rollie and Joanna. Rollie stared at Knox, and for a moment, Knox's face drained of color.

He eyes formed cold, hard slits. His lips tightened into one menacing line.

Rollie kept eye contact until Knox composed himself enough to address the crowd.

Rollie stood as did Joanna, and they linked arms and walked out.

"I thought I would faint," Joanna said as they walked through the lobby.

"You're doing fine," Rollie said.

Outside, they went to the valet parking area and Rollie handed his ticket to the driver.

After the driver went for the car, Karl appeared behind Rollie and hissed, "You son of a bitch."

Rollie and Joanna turned around and faced Karl.

"May I help you?" Rollie said.

"I can't wait for Knox to want you dead, you fucking prick," Karl said.

"Such language," Rollie said.

Knox looked at Joanna. "And who's this cunt?" he said.

Rollie took one step forward off his left foot and kicked Karl in the balls with his right foot.

Karl collapsed to the ground.

Rollie's car arrived.

"Shall we go," Rollie said to Joanna.

They entered the car as Karl stood up, and at that moment, Teal appeared and waved his badge in Karl's face.

"See, there he is," Rollie said and merged into traffic.

• • •

Rollie served coffee to Teal and tea to Joanna in the living room.

"He was madder than a drowning hen," Teal said.

"I expect so," Rollie said.

"Why'd you kick him anyway?" Teal said.

"He called Joanna a rather nasty name," Rollie said.

"I'm still shaking," Joanna said.

"Well, did you learn anything?" Teal said.

"Yeah," Rollie said. "Knox is not going to let anything come between him and the governorship. I saw it in his eyes, on his face, how much he loves an adoring crowd. I also saw a look of total hate and rage when he spotted us in the audience. If I had even a slight doubt before that Knox murdered his wife, I don't anymore."

Teal sighed. "I have to go home," he said and stood up. "And Rollie, watch your back."

After Teal left, Rollie and Joanna sat at the patio table in the backyard.

"What do you think Knox will do now?" Joanna said.

"Make some calls about harassment," Rollie said. "Maybe contact me directly."

"That man was very frightening," Joanna said. "And much bigger than you. Who is he, do you know?"

"His name is Karl Clapper," Rollie said. "An ex-cop—a bad ex-cop—and Knox's driver."

"Driver? He looked like a mobster."

"One and the same in this case," Rollie said.

"What you did, you could have been hurt," Joanna said. "He's even bigger than Knox."

"The goal was to judge Knox's reaction, and he provided the answer," Rollie said. "The next move is his."

"I don't think Knox will stop at some phone calls," Joanna said.

"Anything he does now just makes him look more guilty," Rollie said. "He'll discuss it with his lawyers, they will make the calls and Knox will stay quiet because he won't want to risk any bad publicity. You saw and heard that crowd. You saw the way he fed off them. He's not going to do anything to risk his election."

"After I go home, what are you going to do next?" Joanna said.

"Nothing until I return from London," Rollie said. "Give him a week to stew in his own juice and let his lawyers do their thing. The next move is his."

"Speaking of returning, I have to go home tomorrow," Joanna said. "I have to get ready for the new school year in three weeks. We start a bit earlier than in New York."

"The girls will miss you," Rollie said.

"What about you, Rollie? Will you miss me?" Joanna said.

"I'm not over losing my wife yet," Rollie said. "If I was, the answer would be yes."

"Fair enough," Joanna said.

"Fair enough," Rollie said.

"I better get some sleep," Joanna said. "I have a long drive tomorrow."

"Goodnight, Joanna," Rollie said.

Joanna stood and walked to the kitchen sliding door.

"Joanna," Rollie said.

She paused and looked at Rollie.

"Gloria was right, you do look beautiful," Rollie said.

Joanna smiled, opened the door, and went inside.

Rollie sat and thought for a while. What he saw tonight in Knox was true violence, and even depthless capacity for the same.

But there was something more.

Rollie saw fear in the man's eyes.

Fear made a man do things he wouldn't ordinarily do.

Rollie wondered what fear would cause Knox to do.

The real question was: how far was John Knox willing to go to keep his secret and win the election?

"Time will tell," Rollie said aloud.

CHAPTER TWENTY-NINE

The girls took special care making breakfast for Joanna. Afterward, when it was time for her to leave, Gloria cried, Giselle misted up, and even Grace showed her emotions as they hugged Joanna at her car.

While the girls composed themselves, Rollie did the dishes.

When the girls had regrouped, they sat at the kitchen table and watched Rollie dry and stack dishes.

"Dad, you let her go," Grace said.

Rollie placed the dishes in the cupboard and turned to the girls.

"She had to go home," he said. "She has school in a few weeks."

"That's not what we mean," Grace said.

"I know what you mean, and we're going to London tomorrow," Rollie said. "Unless you want to be left behind with a house sitter, I suggest you zip it, and go make sure you're ready."

Before Rollie could put the silverware in the drawer, the girls had abandoned the table.

•   •   •

Rollie spent the afternoon at his desk, detailing the Knox event from last night.

He called Teal at his office.

"Any blowback from last night?" Rollie said.

"Not yet," Teal said. "I expect soon, though."

"I'm off to London in the morning, but call anytime with news," Rollie said.

"Pip, pip, cheerio, and all that," Teal said.

"Just call me," Rollie said.

"Don't forget your *brolly*," Teal said.

After Teal, Rollie called Gitter and Kline's office.

"I'm glad you called," Gitter said. "All set for London?"

"Yes. Besides reports, I'll be recording the depositions," Rollie said. "What I need is my contact name in London."

"Inspector Joe Charles," Gitter said. "Take down the address and phone number."

Rollie recorded the address on his cell phone and in his notebook as a backup.

After that, he changed and did an hour on the step climber. Joanna called just as he finished.

"I'm home," she said.

"Easy trip?" Rollie said.

"Yes, but tiresome," Joanna said. "Have you heard anything as yet?"

"Quiet as a church mouse."

"Rollie, thank you for making me feel so welcome, you and the girls," Joanna said.

"If the girls had their way, you'd be their new step-mom," Rollie said.

"And how do you feel about that?" Joanna said.

"A topic for another day," Rollie said.

"I suppose," Joanna said. "Good luck in London."

"Thanks," Rollie said. "I'll call you if anything with Knox breaks."

After hanging up with Joanna, Rollie took a shower and changed. He found the girls in the living room, watching a movie.

"If this dog dies, I'll scream," Gloria said.

"Go ahead and scream," Rollie said.

"Dad!" Gloria said.

"We have to get up at 4:00 and leave by 5:00, so we'll eat out tonight," Rollie said. "Get changed and be ready in thirty minutes."

"Do they have pizza in London?" Gloria said.

"I suppose so," Rollie said.

"Can we get pizza tonight just in case?" Gloria said.

"Grace, Giselle?" Rollie said.

"Okay with us," Grace said.

"Thirty minutes," Rollie said.

Rollie drove to The Roma for two large brick oven pizzas with garlic rolls.

"Each of you has an alarm clock, set it for 4:00," Rollie said. "We don't want to be late."

"Dad, thank you for bringing us," Grace said.

"You're very welcome," Rollie said.

"I wish Joanna could go," Gloria said.

"Don't start," Giselle said.

•   •   •

The girls were in bed by 8:30. Rollie went to his office to pack up his tape recorder, documents, and notes.

He locked all the Knox documents in the wall safe on the back wall of the garage office, turned out the lights, and went to bed.

For the first time in weeks, he didn't think about Knox before drifting off to sleep.

CHAPTER THIRTY

There was time for breakfast sandwiches before boarding the plane. They took off on time, and once the pilot announced it was clear to use electronics, the girls, all seated together, watched a movie.

Rollie used his laptop to get some work done. He checked the major New York newspapers for stories on Knox.

One story hailed the fact that Knox had already raised one hundred million in his CPAC for the election and it was still fifteen months away.

Those opposed to Knox were being painted as bitter, angry people clinging to their prejudices.

One opinion piece made comparisons to JFK's Camelot-type campaign. Another said that Knox was quickly becoming the political darling of the country, a hint at a run for the White House down the road.

Ridiculous questions were asked by so-called reporters, such as, where did Knox get his perfect haircuts, and how did he manage to never sweat even on the hottest days and under the hottest lights?

On the flip side, Rollie found a story against Knox for governor. The author of the Op-Ed wrote that Knox was exactly what New York didn't need. With his perfect hair and manicured fingernails, Knox came off as just another baby-kissing, phony politician when, what New York really needed was strong leadership. The author of the article also cited how Knox completely fell apart, by his own admission, after the death of his wife on 9/11, asking the question of how well Knox would hold up under another emergency.

Rollie closed his laptop and took a look at the girls. All three were asleep in their seats.

He opened his briefcase and removed reports on the Broadway actor from London. His trial would be held there and Gitter and Kline and their staff would be allowed to represent him, provided a barrister served as an advisor.

The trial would receive global attention, of that, there was no doubt. Reporters from England, America, and from just about everywhere would cover the trial of the three-time TONY Award–winner, who also won an Emmy, a Golden Globe, and had been nominated for an Oscar.

Rollie read through the evidence.

It was circumstantial and weak, at best. Even the accuser's statement was all hearsay without any real evidence to back up her claim.

Statements from local actors and crew all testified to the Broadway actor's crude behavior and sexism toward women, but nobody actually witnessed him do anything except talk.

That said, many a criminal case has been won on circumstantial evidence.

Rollie ordered a ginger ale and thought about that for a while.

The evidence against Knox was all circumstantial, so far. At a grand jury hearing, his lawyers would tear the evidence to shreds, even the phone call. The real threat to Knox came in the way of negative publicity, that hint of scandal that all politicians feared.

So maybe Joanna was right, maybe keeping Knox from becoming governor was victory enough.

Like trying Al Capone for tax evasion—the government settled for what they could get.

Halfway across the Atlantic, the girls woke up to eat turkey and hummus sandwiches for lunch. Then they watched another movie.

Rollie kept busy writing questions and making notes, and before he knew it, the pilot announced their approach to Heathrow Airport.

The girls buzzed with excitement at the landing. After clearing customs and retrieving their luggage, they went outside to order a taxi.

"Why is it so dark?" Gloria said.

"Because here, it's ten o'clock at night, remember?" Rollie said.

Their hotel was the London Marriot where Rollie had reserved a suite for the five-day stay. The rooms were bright, cheerful, and well-furnished.

"Shall we order dinner while we unpack?" Rollie said.

"It's eleven o'clock at night," Grace said.

"To your stomach, it's only 6:00," Rollie said. "Check the room service menu."

The girls opted for fish and chips. Room service arrived just as they finished unpacking.

"Wait a minute," Gloria said. "These are French fries."

"Not in England," Rollie said. "Here, they're chips."

"Well, what do they call potato chips, then?" Gloria said.

"Crisps," Rollie said.

"Potato crisps?" Gloria said.

After they finished dinner and room service took the trolley away, Rollie suggested watching television for a while.

"Dad, it's almost 1:00 in the morning," Grace said.

"What time do you usually go to bed?" Rollie said.

"10:00, 10:30," Grace said.

"Back home, it's only 9:00," Rollie said. "It's takes a few days to adjust to the jet lag."

They watched a British sitcom and a sci-fi show set in the future, and around 10:30 New York time, everybody turned in for the night.

•   •   •

"Why do I feel like I've been in a car wreck?" Gloria said as they sat down to breakfast the next morning in the hotel suite.

"Jet lag," Rollie said.

"What did you order?" Grace said as they sat down at the table.

"An English Sunday breakfast," Rollie said. "Eggs, bacon, sausage, toast, hash browns and orange juice."

"I think Denny's calls it the Grand Slam," Grace said.

"Eat up, and then I'll be gone for about an hour," Rollie said.

After breakfast, Rollie converted some money into pounds and took a taxi to the police station to meet Inspector Joe Charles.

After introducing himself to an officer in the lobby, Rollie met Charles in his second-floor office.

Charles was in his late fifties and wore a proper British suit.

Charles had a typical London accent that was pleasing to Rollie's American ear. The site chosen for the depositions was the interrogation room at police headquarters. Present would be the prosecuting attorney, Rollie, the witnesses, and Charles. The time was scheduled between 10:00 a.m. and 5:00 p.m., with a one-hour break for lunch.

"Very good, Inspector," Rollie said. "I shall see you at 10:00."

Rollie took a cab back to the hotel and met the girls in the lobby.

"You girls have had plenty of time to pick out what you want to see, so name it," Rollie said.

"Dad, they drive on the wrong side of the road," Gloria said.

"That's what they say about us," Rollie said.

The first stop was Westminster, and then Big Ben, followed by the House of Parliament on the Thames River. After that came Buckingham Palace.

And after that came lunch. They found a local restaurant, and Rollie ordered a traditional dish called bangers and mash, a dish of sausages, mashed potatoes and gravy.

After lunch they went to visit the London Eye, a spectacular Ferris wheel that afforded amazing views of London.

There was still time for one more stop, and they chose Saint Paul's Cathedral, a magnificent church that has stood since the 17th century. From there, they returned to the hotel where the exhausted girls limped to dinner in the hotel dining room.

Rollie ordered the roast dinner, and afterward, the girls went to their rooms and he didn't see them again until morning.

The next day, they went with a more traditional breakfast of bacon and eggs, and then Rollie took the girls with him to a bank to convert some money.

In the bank, Rollie gave Grace two hundred pounds and had her wear the money belt under her shirt.

"How much is a pound?" Grace said.

"According to the bank, about a dollar and thirty cents for every pound note," Rollie said. "Grace, stick close together, and text me every two hours. No exceptions."

"I will," Grace said.

"Giselle, Gloria—Grace is in charge. No arguments," Rollie said. "Have a good time, and Grace, every two hours."

After the girls headed off on their own, Rollie hailed a cab to police headquarters.

CHAPTER THIRTY-ONE

All told, their were nine depositions scheduled over a three day period. Five of the witnesses were men.

Besides Rollie, the prosecutor, Charles, and the witness, a court reporter was on hand to record the depositions.

No one objected to Rollie's use of his tape recorder.

The first witness deposition started at 10:30 and ended at noon.

Then there was a one-hour lunch break.

At 1:30, the next witness gave her deposition, which lasted until 3:00.

That was followed by thirty minutes for tea and biscuits.

From 3:30 until five o'clock, the third witness gave his deposition.

Before hailing a cab, Rollie called Grace and told her to meet him at the hotel at six o'clock.

Over a dinner of pot roast, British-style, the girls filled Rollie in on their adventures of the day.

"This pound thing can be a bit tricky, but I think I got the hang of it," Grace said.

"So, what's on the agenda for tomorrow?" Rollie said.

"The Natural History Museum, the Tate Modern Museum, and the Tower Bridge," Grace said.

"I suggest an early night tonight, or the jet lag will catch up to you tomorrow," Rollie said.

. . .

The next day was a repeat of the first, with three depositions taken.

At dinner, the girls again shared their adventures.

The third day was more of the same, and Rollie thanked Inspector Charles and the court reporter, who told Rollie a copy of the transcripts would be delivered to his hotel in the morning.

In the morning, after breakfast, they took a cab to Heathrow for their noon flight home. While the girls talked about all the things they saw and did, Rollie read the transcripts.

On the flight, he made dozens of pages of notes on a legal pad.

. . .

The first thing Rollie did when they got home was call Gitter and Kline.

"Can you have your client in your office at 11:00 tomorrow morning?" Rollie said. "I'd like to discuss the depositions with him before I proceed with the witnesses in New York."

"We can," Kline said. "How did it go in London?"

"Eye-opening," Rollie said. "We'll talk about it tomorrow."

After Gitter and Kline, Rollie called Teal at his office.

"'Allo chum," Teal said.

"Never mind that, anything happening with Knox I should know about?" Rollie said.

"Knox is flaming-mad about your surprise appearance at his little fundraiser," Teal said. "His lawyers called Andrews again, wanting a restraining order against you. Andrews told them there was no cause. Knox's lawyers took it to a judge, who told them the same thing."

"That must have made Knox even angrier," Rollie said.

"Foaming-at-the-mouth pissed-off, would be my guess," Teal

said. "But all is quiet on the Knox front at the moment."

"Thanks, Bill," Rollie said.

"That's it? Thanks Bill?" Teal said.

"I'll take you to lunch this week—how's that?" Rollie said.

"Make it Friday," Teal said. "Friday is pastrami day at the diner."

"I'll pick you up at noon," Rollie said.

After hanging up with Teal, Rollie found the girls napping in their rooms. To their time clocks, it was after midnight. He woke them up and told them they were eating out tonight.

Reluctantly, they changed and Rollie drove them to the family diner on Queens Boulevard.

After dinner, they were back in bed by eight o'clock.

Knox's lawyers wanted a restraining against him and were refused. Knox must be stewing over that one.

It was time to light a fire under John Knox and see what burned.

CHAPTER THIRTY-TWO

Rollie met Gitter, Kline, and the Broadway actor in the conference room. The actor's name was Jack Ross. He was tall, handsome, and had disheveled-looking hair that was by design.

His net worth was forty million dollars.

He never married, but he was always seen in the company of beautiful women.

"I have nine transcripts from witnesses in London," Rollie said. "Stage hands, bit players, and hotel workers."

Ross looked at Rollie. He was fifty-two years old and had the good looks of a Richard Burton type. His hard-drinking and partying reputation followed him wherever he went.

So did his personal driver.

"I know all this, but I never raped that woman," Ross said.

"I believe you," Rollie said. "None of the witness claimed to have seen you or the woman together except for on stage, and her part was so small they barely remember her at all. Mostly what they remember is your outrageous behavior, filthy language, drinking, and disdain for women."

"What are you saying, exactly?" Ross said.

"The hotel, while they remember you vividly, has no recollection of a woman ever visiting your room," Rollie said.

"That's what I told the damn London police," Ross said.

"Now why don't you tell me?" Rollie said.

"Tell you what?" Ross said.

"The real reason she made those charges against you," Rollie said.

"The play was scheduled for a three-month hiatus this fall," Ross said. "I'm signed to do a film with a forty-five day shoot. She wanted a juicy part in the film. The problem is she can't act, sing, or dance."

"So, you told her no?" Rollie said.

"As did the director, producer, and casting director," Ross said. "So, if she can't get rich and famous one way, she'll do it another."

"Mr. Ross, why was your personal driver in London with you?" Rollie said.

"To drive me around," Ross said.

"Your hotel is one block from the theater," Rollie said. "He stayed in your suite rather than get a room of his own, and he was with you every second of the day. Why not just admit that you're gay and blow a great big hole in the prosecutor's case?"

Next to Rollie, Gitter and Kline gasped.

"And throw away my entire career?" Ross said.

"Thirty years ago, maybe," Rollie said. "Not today. Today, nobody would bat an eye, believe me."

Ross looked at Gitter and Kline. "He's right," Gitter said. "Just look at the major stars that have come out, and nobody cares."

Ross nodded. He said Rollie was one hell of a detective.

∙   ∙   ∙

From his office, Rollie called Joanna.

"Back from London?" Joanna said.

"My body is, my mind is still over there," Rollie said.

"Jet lag?"

"The girls are down for the count," Rollie said. He asked Joanna if she checked the website that listed personal belongings recovered from the victims of 9/11.

"Many times."

"And?"

"Not a thing of Julia's is on the recovery list, of course."

"What if something was?" Rollie said.

"I don't understand," Joanna said.

"Say something of hers was claimed, wouldn't that just confuse the hell out of him?" Rollie said.

"It would, but what?" Joanna said.

"Is there something of hers that he might remember?" Rollie said. "After all, he did get rid of all her stuff, but he must remember certain things."

"Wait, I know just the thing," Joanna said. "A week before she died, Julia had a conference for her job. She borrowed a string of pearls from me and never got the chance to return them. He might remember those."

"Can you describe them?"

"I can do better than that; I have a photo of them."

"Email it to me," Rollie said.

"What are you going to do with it?" Joanna said.

"Show it to him," Rollie said. "Rattle his cage a bit. Get him to thinking about what else he might have overlooked."

"It sounds dangerous," Joanna said.

"So is jaywalking," Rollie said. "It's time to turn up the heat on John Knox."

"I'll send it now. Just promise me you'll be careful," Joanna said.

"I will. Don't worry."

After hanging up with Joanna, Rollie went to the kitchen where Giselle and Gloria were starting dinner.

"Where's Grace?" Rollie said.

"In her room," Giselle said. "She said her stomach hurts."

Rollie went to Grace's room, followed by Giselle and Gloria. The light was out and Rollie flicked the switch.

Grace was in bed.

"What is it?" Rollie said.

"My stomach, Dad," Grace said.

She was covered in sweat as she touched her left side. "Here," she said.

"I'll help you change. I'm taking you to the hospital," Rollie said.

"Umm, Dad, we'll help her change," Giselle said. "Because of, you know."

"I'll get the car," Rollie said.

●　　　●　　　●

Rollie drove to the emergency room at Queens General Hospital. Grace was in considerable pain, and he carried her in.

A nurse quickly approached them.

"Her appendix," Rollie said.

The nurse grabbed a wheelchair, and Rollie set Grace into the seat. "Giselle, Gloria, go with your sister while I check her in," Rollie said.

Rollie spent fifteen minutes at the emergency room check-in counter, and then found Giselle and Gloria standing in the hallway outside a closed room.

"A doctor and nurse are in with her," Giselle said.

Rollie knocked on the door, opened and stepped inside. "I'm her father," he said.

The doctor walked to Rollie. "Acute appendicitis," the doctor said. "I've sent for a surgeon and ordered an operating room."

. . .

"Why is this taking so long?" Gloria said.

"It hasn't been that long," Rollie said. "Only an hour."

"What if…?" Giselle said.

"It's just her appendix," Rollie said. "She'll be home in two days."

"How long is she going to be in there?" Gloria said.

"I waited seventeen hours for her to be born, I can wait a few hours for her appendix," Rollie said.

"Seventeen hours?" Giselle said.

"Thirteen for you, ten for Gloria," Rollie said. "Come on. Let's get some dinner in the cafeteria."

Rollie took them to the hospital cafeteria where they selected burgers with fries, ginger ale, and pie for dessert.

At a table, Giselle said, "You knew it was her appendix right away, Dad. How?"

"I went through it with your mother," Rollie said. "Before any of you were born, she woke up one night in terrible pain, and I rushed her to the hospital and she had it out."

"Grace is going to be okay, right?" Gloria said.

"I expect she'll be coming home in two days," Rollie said.

Back in the waiting room, the surgeon came to see them. "Everything went well," he said. "She'll sleep now until morning. Come back then."

"She's okay?" Gloria said.

The surgeon smiled. "Yeah, she's okay," he said.

. . .

After Giselle and Gloria stumbled into bed, Rollie went to his office to check emails. Joanna had sent him a photograph in a document.

The photograph was of Joanna and Julia at a family function. They were standing together with arms linked. Around Joanna's neck was a string of pearls.

Rollie enlarged the pearls, saved it and printed it. "For you, John Knox," he said aloud.

CHAPTER THIRTY-THREE

Grace was watching television in her room when Rollie, Giselle, and Gloria walked in.

"So, how long did you have a pain in your side?" Rollie said.

"Since the second day in London," Grace said. "I didn't want to spoil anything."

Rollie nodded. "That's what your mother said," he said. "Giselle, Gloria, don't be a dope like your sister. If you're sick, you tell me."

"Can we see your stitches?" Gloria said.

Grace removed the covers and lifted her gown to show a small incision on her left side.

"It's not very big," Gloria said.

"The doctor said I'll have a scar," Grace said. "But it will fade after a while."

"When are you coming home?" Giselle said.

"Good question," Rollie said. "I'll find out."

Rollie went to the nurse's station and they paged the attending doctor. He told Rollie that they wanted to make sure Grace had no infection before clearing her for release. If she didn't develop any infections, she could go home in forty-eight hours.

Rollie returned to the room. "Forty-eight hours," he said.

"Two more days in here?" Grace said.

The doctor entered the room, along with a nurse. "We'll need a moment," he said.

"We'll be back later," Rollie said.

Rollie drove to his bank where he deposited a check from Gitter and Kline for thirty-two thousand dollars.

At home, Giselle and Gloria watched a movie, while Rollie went to his office.

There was a message on his phone from Gitter and Kline. He returned the call and got Kline on the phone.

"Rollie, we'll be on the four o'clock cable news this afternoon," Kline said. "Ross's coming out party. I hope you'll watch."

"I will," Rollie said.

"We hope this will be enough to cancel the trial in London," Kline said. "I expect to hear from them later tonight."

"And here?" Rollie said.

"After today, the DA will probably dismiss the grand jury," Kline said.

"Call me if you need me," Rollie said.

After hanging up with Kline, Rollie went to the living room. "Let's go see your sister," he said.

·   ·   ·

As they walked along the hallway to Grace's room, Gloria said, "Do you think she's feeling better?"

Just outside her room, they heard Grace say, "I can't eat this, it's slop."

"I'd say she's feeling better," Rollie said.

They entered the room and Grace said, "Dad, look what they expect me to eat. I don't even know what this is."

"Hold that thought, honey, I'll be right back," Rollie said.

He went to the nurse's station down the hall. "My daughter,

Grace Finch, can she leave the room for a few minutes?"

"There is a visiting room down the hall to the left, you can sit in there," the nurse said.

Rollie returned to the room. "Grace, you can go to the visiting room with us and I'll get you something from the cafeteria," he said.

"In this gown?" Grace said. "My rear end is hanging out."

"She is a lot of trouble," Gloria said.

"Hop in the wheel chair," Rollie said.

"No looking," Grace said as she left the bed and sat in the wheelchair.

"Alright, girls, follow me," Rollie said.

Rollie pushed the wheelchair to the visitor's room. "I'll run down and get you something," Rollie said.

"Get me a burger with fries, and some chicken, and a vanilla shake," Grace said. "And something for dessert."

"Be right back," Rollie said.

He returned twenty minutes later with a tray loaded with a burger, fries, chicken fingers, a slice of apple pie, and a milk shake.

Grace gobbled everything up as if she hadn't eaten in a week.

"I'm going to see a doctor," Rollie said. He went to the nurse's station and asked to see the attending physician. He was told one would meet him in the room in a few minutes.

He returned to Grace and wheeled her back to the room to wait.

The doctor came in and gave Grace a quick examination. "I'd say four o'clock tomorrow afternoon, she's all yours, Mr. Finch."

After the doctor left, Grace said, "I need clothes. I can't go home in pajamas."

"What do you need?" Rollie said.

"Jeans, a blouse, socks, sneakers and..." Grace said.

"And what?" Rollie said.

"Dad," Grace said.

"Never mind, we'll get them," Giselle said.

Riding down in the elevator, Rollie said, "Get what?"

"Panties and a bra, Dad," Giselle said. "You have three daughters, how could you not know that?"

•   •   •

Rollie watched the Ross press conference on his computer in his office. By the reaction of reporters in attendance, you would think the Queen of England had announced she was a transvestite.

Once they got into the Q & A, Rollie turned it off and called Teal at his office.

"Did you see the Ross conference?" Rollie said.

"Most of it," Teal said. "Your handiwork?"

"A good part of it," Rollie said. "How are things on the western front?"

"If you mean Knox, I haven't heard a word since his lawyers went batshit crazy on Andrews," Teal said.

"I expect that to change in a few days," Rollie said.

"Why?"

"I'll explain as soon as I figure out the details," Rollie said. "In the meantime, Grace had her appendix out yesterday."

"How is she?"

"Home tomorrow with a scar to brag about," Rollie said.

"Good. Didn't Georgia have hers out?" Teal said.

"Before the girls were born," Rollie said. "I'll call you after I figure out my next move with Knox."

After hanging up with Teal, Rollie found Giselle and Gloria watching television.

"Girls, should we cook dinner tonight, or get a big bucket of chicken?" he said.

CHAPTER THIRTY-FOUR

Grace emerged from the bathroom fully dressed and ready to go.

Rollie had the wheelchair at the ready.

"Oh, come on, Dad," Grace said.

"Hospital rule," Rollie said. "It's just until we reach the exit door."

Once they were in the car, Rollie said, "I need to stop at the drugstore to pick up your prescription."

"For what?" Grace said.

"Prevent infection," Rollie said.

"What I need is food," Grace said. "Breakfast was terrible and I skipped lunch."

"When we get home, I'll drop you girls off and then go to the pharmacy," Rollie said.

When he got settled in back home, Rollie went to his office and looked at the photograph of the string of pearls.

He took a chance and called Joanna's cell number.

"Hi Rollie, I was wondering when you would call," she said.

"Things got a bit delayed," Rollie said. "Grace had her appendix taken out..."

"What? How is she?"

"She's home. She'll be fine," Rollie said.

"Thank God for that," Joanna said.

"What I wanted to ask you is, how sure are you that Knox will recognize those pearls?" Rollie said.

"Remember the photo I sent you?"

"I'm looking at it right now," Rollie said.

"Knox took that photo," Joanna said.

"Very good," Rollie said.

"What are you planning?"

"I'm not sure yet," Rollie said. "I'll call you as soon as I am."

Pizza was delivered for dinner and Rollie paid the driver and brought them to the kitchen. "Girls, dinner," he said.

Grace entered the kitchen first. "I could eat a bear," she announced.

"Did you take your prescription?" Rollie said.

"It says 'take with food'," Grace said.

"Dig in and then take your pill," Rollie said.

Two large pizzas and a dozen garlic rolls were gone in the blink of an eye.

"Grace, you look tired. I want you to get in bed. Giselle, Gloria, sit with her until she's asleep," Rollie said. "I'll take care of the kitchen."

Rollie did the dishes, dried and stacked, then went to Grace's room. Giselle and Gloria were in chairs beside the bed.

"She's down," Gloria said.

"Okay, you can watch TV until 10:30," Rollie said.

Rollie went to the kitchen to grab a ginger ale. The girls followed him.

"Hey, Dad, we're you worried?" Giselle said.

"Your sister is a strong girl," Rollie said. "I never doubted for a minute she'd be home in two days."

"We'll be in my room for a while," Gloria said.

Rollie went to his office and used his computer to check Knox's website. According to his posted schedule, he would be in Albany for the next week.

Tomorrow. He'd call Knox tomorrow.

.　　.　　.

Always a light sleeper, Rollie heard a noise coming from the kitchen and he got out of bed to investigate.

Grace was at the table with a glass of milk and a bag of chocolate chip cookies.

"And we're out of bed because…?" Rollie said as he grabbed a glass and filled it with milk.

"I was hungry," Grace said.

"You had five slices of pizza and four garlic rolls not five hours ago," Rollie said.

"I'm a growing girl, Dad," Grace said.

Rollie grabbed a cookie and dunked it in milk.

"Dad, I was scared," Grace said.

"I wasn't," Rollie said. "I went through the exact same thing with your mother."

"She had her appendix out?"

"Before you guys were born," Rollie said.

"That's how you knew?"

"That's how I knew."

"What's going on, why are you in the kitchen?" Giselle said as she entered, rubbing her eyes.

"We are having milk and cookies," Rollie said.

Giselle grabbed a glass just as Gloria sleepily wandered in behind her. "How come everybody is awake?" she said.

"We're having milk and cookies," Giselle said.

Gloria grabbed a glass and sat at the table and grabbed a cookie.

"I think we're going to need to open another bag," Rollie said.

CHAPTER THIRTY-FIVE

"Detective Rollie Finch calling for Lieutenant Governor Knox," Rollie said.

"Do you have an appointment?" a female on the other end of the line said.

"I wasn't aware there was such a thing as needing an appointment for a phone call," Rollie said.

"Oh yes, otherwise, Mr. Knox would be on the phone all day, and never get anything else done."

"Ask Mr. Knox if he has time for a call from Detective Finch," Rollie said. "I'm sure he does."

"Please hold."

Rollie timed how long he was on hold, listening to horrible elevator music. Exactly twelve minutes.

"You have some fucking pair of balls calling me at the office," Knox said when he came on the line.

"I hope this call isn't being recorded for quality control," Rollie said.

"Fuck you. What do you want?" Knox said.

"Your wrists in handcuffs, but I'll settle for a face-to-face," Rollie said.

"And give me one good reason why I should allow you to see me," Knox said.

"Because if you don't, I will take everything I have and bring it right to the *New York Times*," Rollie said. "Oh, nobody will come to arrest you, but you might lose ten points in the polls. That's a tough nut to win back, especially with the women's vote, if they think you killed your wife."

Knox sighed. "When?"

"Say, Friday noon," Rollie said.

"Say I agree, what do you want?" Knox said.

"Just to talk," Rollie said.

"You have noon to 12:30," Knox said.

"Fair enough," Rollie said. "Until then."

Rollie left his office and found the girls watching a movie on television.

"Gloria, you come with me to the grocery store," he said. "Giselle, stay with your sister. We won't be long."

Riding to the store, Gloria said, "How come you never pick Giselle to go to the store?"

"Because she's fifteen and you're not," Rollie said. "Grace will put up with being baby-sat by a fifteen-year-old, but not a thirteen-year-old."

"I get it," Gloria said.

"And besides, I need somebody to…" Rollie said.

"Push the cart," Gloria said. "Yeah, I know."

After an hour, they left the grocery store with a full cart. They loaded the back seat of the Buick with bags, and before Rollie got behind the wheel, Grace called his cell phone.

"Dad, the doctor called," she said. "He called in a renewal on my prescription."

"I'll get it," Rollie said.

The pharmacy was one block away. "Stay in the car, I'll be right back," Rollie said to Gloria after he drove to the pharmacy.

Rollie was gone not five minutes and when he returned, a boy of about eighteen was leaning into the car, talking to Gloria.

Rollie approached the boy. "And you want what exactly?" he said.

The boy turned around. "Mr. Finch, it's me, James Seymour, from up the block."

Rollie looked at James. "You're at least eighteen. Gloria is a bit young for you, don't you think?"

James actually blushed. "Um, no sir," he said. "I mean, what I mean is, I'm in Grace's class. I was just asking how she is. I heard she was sick in the hospital."

"She had her appendix out and she's fine," Rollie said.

"Is she going to the dance in two weeks?" James said.

"You should ask her that," Rollie said.

"I mean, what I mean is, can I ask her to be my date for the dance?" James said.

"Again, you should ask her that," Rollie said. "Do you know where we live?"

"Yes sir, right up the street from me."

"Stop by around five o'clock and ask her then," Rollie said.

"Yes sir, I will. Thank you, sir," James said.

Driving home, Rollie said, "Don't tell your sister about this."

"Why not?" Gloria said.

"Because it's more fun for the girl when it's a surprise," Rollie said.

• • •

"Bill, it's Rollie. I'm meeting Knox on Friday at noon in Albany," Rollie said.

"Because?" Teal said.

The garage door was open for ventilation, and Rollie spotted James walking past.

"Hold on, Bill, some kid is here to ask Grace for a date," Rollie said. "In fact, let me call you back."

"Rollie, I…" Teal said as Rollie hung up.

Rollie went inside just in time to open the door.

"Hello sir, it's five o'clock," James said.

"And so it is," Rollie said.

James looked at Rollie.

"Did you come to ask me to the dance or my daughter?" Rollie said.

"You said… I'm here to see Grace, sir," James said.

"Quit tripping over your tongue and follow me," Rollie said.

James followed Rollie to the kitchen where the girls were reading from Georgia's cookbook.

"Giselle, Gloria, out, Grace has a visitor," Rollie said.

Giselle and Gloria looked at James.

Dressed in pajamas, her hair a mess, Grace looked at Rollie, who said, "James, no hanky-panky."

"What's…?" James said.

"Giselle, Gloria, living room," Rollie said.

Rollie, Giselle, and Gloria went to the living room.

"What's going on?" Giselle said.

"He's asking her to the dance," Gloria said.

"How do you know?" Giselle said.

"He told me," Gloria said.

"He told you?" Giselle said. "Why would he tell you?"

"I don't know. He's kind of stupid," Gloria said.

Grace rushed into the living room. "Dad, Dad, James asked me to be his date to the dance," she said. "I said yes. Is that okay?"

"Yes, it's okay," Rollie said.

Grace kissed Rollie on the cheek, said, "Thanks, Dad," and rushed back to the kitchen.

"You're right, Dad, it is more fun," Gloria said.

"What's more fun," Giselle said.

"Talk amongst yourselves," Rollie said and returned to his office. He stood at the open door and waited.

After a few minutes, James was strolling past and Rollie said, "James, a moment please."

"Yes sir," James said.

"The night of the dance, bring Grace a corsage," Rollie said.

"A corsage?" James said.

"She'll like that very much," Rollie said.

"I will, sir," James said. "That's a flower, right?"

"Yes," Rollie said. "The girl wears it on her left wrist."

"Thanks, Mr. Finch," James said.

Rollie returned to his desk. "When Gloria's right, she's right," he said, and called Teal back.

"Where were we?" Rollie said.

"Some kid is asking Grace for a date," Teal said.

"Before that," Rollie said.

"Albany," Teal said.

"Oh yes," Rollie said. "I'm meeting Knox at his office at noon on Friday."

"What for?" Teal said.

"I'll explain when I take you to lunch tomorrow," Rollie said.

"It better be another steak," Teal said.

"I'll pick you up at noon," Rollie said.

Rollie went to the kitchen where the girls were still browsing through the cookbook.

"So, what shall we have for dinner tonight?" he said.

CHAPTER THIRTY-SIX

"What pearls, what are you talking about?" Teal said.

"How's your steak?" Rollie said.

"Delicious," Teal said. "Now, suppose you tell me what the hell you're talking about."

"How many suspects would you say you've interviewed?" Rollie said.

"Thousands."

"And you can always tell by looking in their eyes," Rollie said. "That's what I want to do when I tell him his wife's pearls were recovered in the rubble; I want to look into his eyes."

"But doesn't that put his wife in the Towers and exonerate him?" Teal said.

"Yup," Rollie said.

Teal smiled. "I want to be like you when I grow up," he said.

"I'll meet you at 8:00 and we'll take your car," Rollie said.

"Why my car?" Teal said.

"Because it's an unmarked police car and I don't want any state troopers bothering us," Rollie said.

Teal nodded. "We should get some dessert," he said.

• • •

From his office, Rollie called Joanna.

"I'm meeting Knox on Friday at his office in Albany," Rollie said.

"Over the pearls?" Joanna said.

"I want to judge his reaction when I tell him they've been recovered," Rollie said.

"But won't he know they weren't?"

"And he can't admit that without admitting his guilt," Rollie said.

"So, what is he going to do?" Joanna said.

"That remains to be seen," Rollie said.

"If he stays true to his colors, he'll get mean," Joanna said.

"I hope so," Rollie said.

"How is Grace?" Joanna said.

"Seemingly back to normal," Rollie said.

"Good."

"I'll call you after I see Knox," Rollie said.

After hanging up with Joanna, Rollie changed into sweats and did an hour on the step climber.

Knox would be backed into a corner over the pearls. If he admitted they were his wife's, it put her in the World Trade Center on 9/11, and exonerated him. But could he look Rollie in the eyes and hide his guilt?

It was a double-edged sword with one edge at Knox's throat.

And Knox was smart enough to know that. Was he smart enough to avoid the pitfalls?

Rollie doubted that. Not Knox's intelligence, but his emotions.

Sooner or later, Knox's emotions would win out, and he would flare up and self destruct.

Rollie wanted to be there to watch that happen.

When the hour was up, Rollie went to take a shower. Then he tossed on clean sweats and found the girls in the kitchen.

"Girls, I have some steak tips marinating in the refrigerator. Get some carrots and baked potatoes going and I'll do the honors on the grill," Rollie said.

Rollie went to the backyard to heat up the grill.

It was a warm, clear August night. The weather would stay warm for another month before October hinted at the winter that was to come.

Georgia wasn't a summer person. Not that she didn't enjoy summer activates with the girls, but she really loved the holidays. Her favorite season started at Thanksgiving, maybe even Halloween, and rolled right through Christmas and New Year's.

The first year after Georgia died, they didn't decorate the house or get a Christmas tree. Instead of gifts, they donated money to the church and Georgia's favorite charity.

What Rollie was leading up to in his mind was inviting Joanna for Christmas.

He wasn't sure how the girls would react to that. They enjoyed her company, but would they consider her coming for Christmas an invasion of their mother's territory?

There were months to think about it.

Rollie centered his mind back on Knox

Grace came out with a platter of steak tips. "Everything else is ready, Dad," she said.

"About fourteen minutes," Rollie said.

While the steak tips sizzled, Rollie thought about what Knox might do. If he swallowed the story about the pearls, it would exonerate him of Joanna's claim.

But…

And there is always a but.

What would his next move be knowing the story about the pearls was a lie?

With a man like Knox, a man who so callously killed and

disposed of his wife, the sky was the limit when it came to what he would or wouldn't do.

As a homicide detective, Rollie had seen the worst of the lot. Serial killers, crimes of passion, those who killed just for the sake of killing, and those who made it a profession.

The very worst of the bunch were those that lacked compunction.

In Rollie's mind, that was the category Knox fit into.

A man without compunction.

The steak tips were done, and Rollie loaded up the tray and carried it into the kitchen.

"Girls, after breakfast tomorrow, we're going shopping," Rollie said.

"For what, Dad?" Grace said.

"Hopefully something I won't regret," Rollie said.

CHAPTER THIRTY- SEVEN

"Why are we taking an Uber? Is something wrong with the car?" Grace said.

"The car is fine," Rollie said.

"Then…?" Grace said.

"The cab is here," Rollie said.

About a mile and a half south on Queens Boulevard was a large used car dealership where the driver dropped them off.

"Are you replacing the Buick?" Grace said.

"I like the Buick," Gloria said.

"Be quiet for a moment," Rollie said. "Grace, having a car is a great responsibility and…"

"Grace is getting a car?" Giselle said.

"If she gets a car, I want a puppy," Gloria said.

"If she gets a puppy, I want a boyfriend," Giselle said.

"Am I getting a car?" Grace said.

"If you don't zip it, none of you are getting anything," Rollie said. "You are to drive your sisters to school and pick them up afterward. You are not to drive the car without telling me in advance. You are to always have your cell phone with you, but are to never use it while driving. Most of all, remember your sisters will be with you, so you drive like their lives depend on it, because they do. Are we clear?"

Grace, a bit overwhelmed, just nodded.

"I still want a puppy," Gloria said.

Rollie looked at her.

"I'll be quiet," Gloria said.

A salesman approached them. "Good morning," he said. "How can I help you?"

"My daughter Grace needs a car," Rollie said. "Nothing older than four years, nothing higher than sixty-thousand miles. No convertibles. Six cylinders and front wheel drive. Giselle, Gloria, go help your sister pick out a car."

"You're not coming?" Grace said.

"It's your car, you pick it," Rollie said.

"Ladies, let me show you what we have," the salesman said.

While the girls and the salesman looked at cars, Rollie called Teal on his cell phone.

"It's two and a half hours to Albany," Rollie said. "I'm meeting Knox at noon. 8:00 might be a bit early. Let's make it 8:30."

"What's all that noise?" Teal said.

"Street traffic," Rollie said. "We're at a used car lot. I'm buying a car for Grace."

"I didn't realize she was that old."

"Eighteen in a few weeks," Rollie said.

"8:30, and don't skimp on the donuts," Teal said.

After hanging up, Rollie walked around and looked at cars and SUVs. He was kicking the tires on a Jeep when they found him and Grace said, "Dad, it's between two cars. Come have a look."

Rollie followed them to a four-year-old Chevy Impala, light blue in color with fifty-six-thousand miles on it. The used price was eighteen-thousand four hundred dollars.

The second car was a Ford Fusion, also four-years-old, silver in color and with just fifty-one-thousand miles on it. The price was nineteen thousand five hundred dollars.

"I can't decide," Grace said.

"There are a couple of factors to consider," Rollie said. "Take them for a test drive so your sisters can see which one has more room in back."

"And the other?" Grace said.

"Which you're more comfortable driving," Rolli4e said. "I'll wait here."

Rollie was looking at the lines on an F-150 when they returned from test driving the Impala, and checking out the cargo capacity on a Dodge Ram when they returned with the Fusion.

"They both have plenty of room in back and they both handle very well," Grace said. "And I still can't decide which."

"I'll knock four hundred off both," the salesman said.

"The Ford is a thousand more, but has five thousand fewer miles on it," Grace said. "Wouldn't it make more sense to go with less miles?"

"Then it's settled," Rollie said. "Let's go in and do the paperwork."

In the office, the salesman said, "How do you want to finance this?"

Rollie took out his checkbook. "Tell me the amount and then call my bank," he said.

A bit later, Grace drove them off the lot in the Fusion.

"I still want a boyfriend," Giselle said from the rear.

"And a puppy," Gloria said.

"Why are you driving so slow?" Giselle said.

"The speed limit on this section of Queens Boulevard is thirty-five," Rollie said.

"She never drives this slow in your car," Gloria said.

Rollie looked at Grace.

"Oops," Gloria said.

"What's our house rule about tattling?" Rollie said.

"The tattler has to do extra chores," Gloria said. "Except we're not in the house, we're in Grace's new car, and I still don't have a puppy."

Rollie had to grin.

"She's got you there, Dad," Giselle said.

When they reached home, Rollie said, "Back it in so you don't have to back out into traffic."

Grace backed the Fusion past Rollie's car into the garage.

"Alright, grab the owner's manual and read every page before lunch," Rollie said.

While Grace read the owner's manual in her room, Rollie called Gloria to his bedroom.

"The car was Grace's eighteenth birthday gift a bit early, so she can take you and Gloria to school," he said.

"I know that, Dad," Gloria said.

"For her sixteenth birthday, I gave Grace her mother's necklace," Rollie said.

"I remember."

"As your sixteenth is right after Grace's, I'm giving you these now," Rollie said and handed Giselle and small box. "Your mother wore these on our wedding day."

Giselle opened the box. "Mom's diamond earrings," she said and started to cry.

In the hallway, Gloria said, "And what do I get?"

"On Saturday, we'll go get you a puppy."

CHAPTER THIRTY-EIGHT

As Teal reached for the last donut in his bag, he said, "Four donuts for a three-hour drive doesn't cut it."

"I haven't touched my two, take one," Rollie said.

With one hand on the wheel, Teal opened Rollie's bag. "These are crullers," he said.

"Skip them," Rollie said. "I made a lunch reservation at the Texas Brazilian Steakhouse for 1:30 anyway," Rollie said.

"Texas Brazilian, huh?" Teal said.

"That should give you plenty of time to digest those donuts," Rollie said.

"Well, we still have two hours to go," Teal said.

"You ate four chocolate donuts in thirty minutes, and you wonder why your wife is serving you lettuce and carrot sticks?" Rollie said.

"Never mind that. What about these pearls?" Teal said.

"My guess is Knox tossed them or sold them when he got rid of his wife's things," Rollie said. "That's not important. What is important is how Knox reacts."

"I'll lay you two-to-one he pops his cork," Teal said.

"I don't think so," Rollie said. "I think he'll stay calm on the outside and go furnace on the inside."

"Let me ask you a question," Teal said. "Are you still working for Joanna Kearns or for yourself? Because it seems to me she can't afford to pay you for the job you're doing."

"I've been working for myself since the second week, Bill," Rollie said. "The old cop in me can't stand to see a man like Knox get away with murder, I suppose."

"That job Andrews offered you," Teal started.

"Assistant Chief of D's," Rollie said. "What about it?"

"I did some checking in the department," Teal said. "A hundred and twenty-five K a year is nothing to sneeze at, plus if you do five years, you'll pension out at three-quarter pay."

"I know, but I have three girls at home, and right now, I work when I want to and I can keep a close eye on them," Rollie said. "I'd have to hire a full-time live-in, and I don't want that. Their mother wouldn't want that either."

"I understand," Teal said. "In your shoes, I'd do the same."

"Reminds me," Rollie said. He took out his cell phone and called home on the hard line. Giselle answered the call.

"Hi, Dad," she said.

"What are you guys up to?" Rollie said.

"Making breakfast," Giselle said.

"I meant for the day," Rollie said. "I won't be home until after 5:00."

"We're looking at dogs online for the squirt, and if it's okay, we're going to the park to play soccer," Giselle said.

"That might be too much for Grace right now," Rollie said. "Her checkup is on Monday."

"Hold on, Dad," Giselle said.

Grace came on the line. "Dad, I'm fine. I feel really good," she said.

"The park is six blocks away, don't drive and make sure you all take your cell phones," Rollie said. "If you feel sick or weak, stop, go home, and call me. Understand?"

"Yes, Dad," Grace said.

"Alright, have fun, but don't overdo it," Rollie said.

Rollie put his cell phone away.

Teal said, "Yeah. In your shoes, with three girls, I probably wouldn't take that job either."

"Exactly."

. . .

Teal parked in the municipal lot a block from Knox's office at the state house office building.

"So, where is this steak house?" Teal said.

"For Christ sake, Bill, can we see Knox first?" Rollie said.

They walked to the state offices where Teal had to check his firearm before being allowed in to see Knox.

Karl met them in the hallway outside Knox's office.

"Well, well, the police captain," Karl said. "Are you taking your little dog for a walk?"

"This is an official visit, Clapper," Teal said. "Kindly step out of the way."

"I'm to escort you to the office," Karl said.

"Now who's the little dog?" Rollie said.

Karl grinned. "I haven't forgotten that kick in the balls," he said.

"And I haven't forgotten kicking you," Rollie said. "Good times."

"Follow me," Karl said.

Karl led them into the offices to a back room and opened the door.

"You wait outside," Teal said.

Knox stood up from behind his desk. "Captain William Teal," he said. "I wondered if Finch would bring you along."

"This is an official visit, so let's get to it," Teal said.

Knox took his chair behind the desk. Rollie and Teal took chairs facing the desk.

"You have twenty-eight minutes," Knox said.

Rollie pulled an envelope from his suit jacket pocket and removed a folded photograph and set it on the desk. "Recognize this?" he said.

"It appears to be a string of white pearls," Knox said.

"That wasn't the question," Rollie said. "The question is do you recognize them?"

"No. Should I?" Knox said.

Rollie removed the second photograph and set it beside the first. Knox looked at the photo of Julia and Joanna, who wore the pearls around her neck.

"How about now?" Rollie said.

"My dearly departed wife and her cunt of a sister," Knox said. "So what?"

"So your ex-sister-in-law loaned those pearls to your wife, and apparently, they were recovered in the Trade Center's rubble," Rollie said. "Evidently, she wore them to the office. They lay unclaimed until recently, when her sister noticed them listed on the unclaimed list. It's amazing how much stuff has never been claimed."

Knox stared at the photographs for many seconds. When he looked up, his eyes were filled with fury and his mouth was a tight, thin line.

The moment of rage passed, Knox's eyes lightened, and he smiled. "Convinced now she died on 9/11?" he said.

"As soon as the pearls are released to the family and tested by NYPD for possible DNA, which should be in her perspiration," Rollie said.

Knox stared at Rollie.

Rollie could see the gears spinning in Knox's brain as Knox tried to figure out the angle Rollie was playing.

"Well, that's it, I guess," Rollie said. "As soon as DNA tests are conducted, feel free to make a public statement," Rollie said. "Or not. Up to you."

Rollie and Teal stood and walked to the door.

"Finch," Knox said.

Rollie and Teal turned around.

"You're a smart fellow," Knox said. "Don't get too smart. I'm a smart fellow, myself."

. . .

"This is the best goddamn steak I ever had," Teal said.

"For sixty dollars a pop, it should be," Rollie said.

"And worth every penny of your money," Teal said.

"So what do you think?" Rollie said.

"The steak fries are perfect," Teal said.

"About Knox."

"Ever see a dog being scolded after they did something wrong that they knew to be wrong?" Teal said. "They have that guilty-dog look in their eyes. I saw that in Knox's eyes."

Rollie nodded. "The question is, what is he going to about it? If he goes public and we admit we were mistaken, he not only looks foolish but it brings up the subject of whether she actually died on 9/11?"

"And if he keeps quiet, he runs the risk of us announcing we believe we found his wife's pearls in the rubble, and that makes him look callous," Teal said. "That 'you're a smart fellow' bullshit, that was a threat."

"I know," Rollie said. "But a threat to do what?"

"Does it matter? Threatening a police officer is a crime," Teal said.

"If you can prove the threat, which we can't," Rollie said. "Being a smart fellow is not illegal."

"This steak is amazing," Teal said.

"Want dessert?" Rollie said.

"Does the Pope pray?" Teal said.

●　　●　　●

Walking back to Teal's car, Rollie spotted Karl standing across the street from the parking garage.

"Don't look now but Herman Munster is eyeballing us," Teal said.

"Knox sent him," Rollie said. "In case we didn't understand his 'smart fellow' threat."

"Are those two donuts still in the car?" Teal said.

●　　●　　●

"The cold-blooded son of a bitch is going to make some kind of move," Teal said.

"He's got his lawyers searching the survival database for unclaimed items," Rollie said.

"And when they find nothing?" Teal said.

"I already checked," Rollie said. "There are three sets of pearl necklaces left unclaimed."

"Let the bastard sweat," Teal said.

CHAPTER THIRTY-NINE

"Dad, I'll need to stop for gas," Grace said. "I only have a half a tank."

"We'll do that before we get on the highway," Rollie said. "First stop is the diner for breakfast."

Grace drove the family to the diner on Queens Boulevard in her Fusion.

As they ate breakfast, they discussed the adoption of a puppy for Gloria. The ASPCA on Long Island had a litter of Beagle puppies up for adoption. The puppies were sixteen weeks old and Gloria had reserved one by phone.

"I don't know where the place is, Dad," Grace said.

"That's what the GPS is for," Rollie said.

After breakfast, Rollie programmed the GPS. The directions had the trip at seventy-five miles and said it would take approximately ninety minutes.

At first, Grace was nervous about taking the Fusion on the highway for the first time, but Rollie told her she'd be fine and that helped.

"Gloria, I know you and your sisters researched dogs extensively, so I'm curious, why a Beagle puppy?" Rollie said.

"They're cute and they don't grow very big and they have a lot of energy," Gloria said. "And they are very loving and loyal."

"All good reasons," Rollie said. "Also, small dogs live much longer than large dogs, so he'll be around longer."

"I read about that, too" Gloria said.

"I have a question for you, Gloria," Rollie said. "Whenever you and Giselle are in Grace's care, what do I always tell her?"

"Responsibility," Gloria said.

Rollie glanced at Grace and she grinned at him.

Forty-five-minutes later, they arrived at the ASPCA in the town of Farmington.

Of the six Beagle puppies, two remained, a brother and sister. The female was cold and showed no interest in Gloria, but the male was on her in an instant.

"The Beagle has chosen," Rollie said. "Let's fill out the adoption papers."

After filling out the papers, which included a promise to send a vet's report within seven days, Rollie paid the adoption fee, and Gloria leashed the Beagle and walked him to the car.

"The manager said he's been leash-trained for at least a month, so that means he's smart," Gloria said.

As soon as Gloria opened the car door, the Beagle jumped into the rear seat.

"Grace, take us home," Rollie said.

• • •

Rollie sat at the backyard patio table with a glass of ginger ale and watched the girls chase the Beagle and a soccer ball around the yard.

The puppy had energy to spare and only stopped when the girls took a break.

The puppy followed Gloria to the table and sat beside her when she took a chair.

"Now that we know he's comfortable, we need to take a ride to the pet store," Rollie said. "Leash him up and let's go."

Grace and Giselle came along for the ride.

At the pet store, they selected a bed, food bowls, puppy food, a new leash, some chew toys, brushes, and dog shampoo.

On the ride home, Rollie said, "Gloria, what are you going to name your newfound buddy?"

"That," Gloria said.

"What?" Rollie said.

"Buddy," Gloria said. "It's perfect."

"Then welcome to the family, Buddy."

.   .   .

Rollie called Teal at his home.

"Bill, it's Rollie."

"It's Saturday—don't you ever take a day off?" Teal said.

"Just curious if you heard any blowback," Rollie said.

"Not yet," Teal said. "My guess is Monday, if at all."

"I'm going to go out on a limb and say he won't go public," Rollie said. "He'll wait for us to make the next move."

"You could be right."

"We got a dog. A Beagle puppy."

"What the hell for?"

"Because Grace got a car, and Giselle got earrings," Rollie said.

"Somehow that connection escapes me," Teal said.

After hanging up with Teal, Rollie called Joanna.

"Rollie, I was just wondering when you would call," she said.

"I thought I'd fill you in on my trip to Albany," Rollie said.

After fifteen minutes or so, Rollie had brought Joanna up to speed.

"Wow, what's he going to do now?" Joanna said.

"Remains to be seen," Rollie said. "He knows we can't arrest him. Yet. We can, however, cost him the election."

"That's the important thing for the moment, keeping that monster out of office," Joanna said.

"There are no limitations on murder, and it will be much easier to build a case for it if he's not elected," Rollie said.

"School starts here in one week," Joanna said. "I'll be making a quick trip to see my mother before it starts. I'll tell her your progress. She'll be very pleased."

"Tell her I said hello," Rollie said.

"I will," Joanna said.

Before dinner, Rollie wrote a very detailed report to himself about the meeting with Knox.

At the end of the report, he made a list of questions titled "Knox's Options."

1. Nothing. Do nothing and wait it out.

2. Try to claim a pearl necklace as his wife's and hold a press conference seeking sympathy from the voting public. All the old pain returning, cry a few tears on TV, blah, blah, blah.

3. Contact the commissioner and claim harassment by NYPD and private detective Rollie Finch.

4. Have his lawyers sue Rollie Finch for slander.

5. Publicly deny the necklace belonged to his wife.

6. Take the offensive and up his campaign speeches and stumping. Alert the public to the false claim brought down upon him by his opponents.

Rollie paused. Bringing the false claim to light was an excellent way to dispel the charge against him. It worked for every politician since the beginning of time, so why not John Knox?

A bit later, dinner was ready. Buddy sat beside Gloria at the table, didn't beg, and finally lay down.

"Don't get him into the habit of begging for scraps," Rollie said, "He won't want his food. That goes for all three of you."

"We know," Gloria said. "And we won't."

"We'll go for ice cream for dessert," Rollie said. "They have a doggie bowl."

CHAPTER FORTY

On Monday morning, Rollie and the girls took Buddy to the vet for his checkup and shots.

"Can we take him to the dog park for a bit so he gets used to it?" Gloria said on the way home from the vet.

"Why not?" Rollie said.

He drove them to the dog park about a half mile from home and sat on a bench with a container of coffee while the girls played with Buddy and introduced him to other dogs.

To Rollie's shock, when his cell phone rang, it was Knox calling directly from Albany.

"Mr. Finch, it's Lieutenant Governor Knox," he said.

"What can I do for you, Mr. Knox?" Rollie said.

"I'll be in Manhattan tomorrow. Let's meet, sit down, and talk this out."

"What time?" Rollie said.

"12:30."

"Your headquarters?"

"Correct."

"I'll see you there," Rollie said.

Rollie called Teal at his office right away.

"I am about to eat a lettuce-and-tomato sandwich for lunch, packed with love by my wife," Teal said.

"No bacon?" Rollie said.

"I haven't seen pig in my house for months," Teal said.

"Why not just go to that diner?" Rollie said.

"My crazy wife checks my wallet before I leave the house and she'll check it again when I get home," Teal said. "She checks ATM statements and debit card withdrawals. She'll know if I cheat. That's why you're always buying for me."

"How would you like a real lunch tomorrow?" Rollie said.

"I'm listening," Teal said.

Buddy bounded his way up to Rollie with a tennis ball in his mouth, and Rollie gave it a long chuck. There went Buddy.

"Knox has made the first move," Rollie said. "I'm meeting him at 12:30 tomorrow in Manhattan to talk."

"Talk?"

"That's what he said," Rollie said.

"Am I invited?"

"Nope, but I figured we can get lunch after and I could fill you in on the good times then," Rollie said.

"Where is this little parley taking place?" Teal said.

"Knox's headquarters on Broadway," Rollie said.

"Not exactly a neutral corner," Teal said.

"I figure you could park on the street, let your presence be known," Rollie said. "And then we can go get lunch afterward."

"Sounds like a plan," Teal said. "What do you think he's going to say?"

"Anything and everything but the truth," Rollie said.

"Meet me in my office at 11:00," Teal said. "I'd like you to wear a wire."

"My guess is Lurch will frisk me for that," Rollie said. "I have a better idea."

"What?"

"I'll show you tomorrow," Rollie said.

After hanging up with Teal, Rollie said, "Girls, time to go home. Buddy looks tuckered out."

• • •

In his office, Rollie went to the back wall, past the step climber, where a large tool chest stood. The chest was designed for auto mechanics, and Rollie had modified it into a type of strongbox.

Besides the built-in combination lock, Rollie had installed a hasp latch with a heavy key-lock.

The key was on his key ring, and he removed the padlock and then opened the combination lock.

Inside the tool chest was a Benelli M-4 shotgun, two Glock pistols, and a massive .357 Magnum revolver, with several speed loaders for the revolver and bricks of ammunition for the rest.

Also on the top shelf was a small, wooden box. Rollie removed the box, closed and locked the safe.

Then he went to the kitchen to help the girls with dinner.

"Dad, Buddy needs a walk around ten o'clock," Gloria said.

"No problem," Rollie said. "We'll walk him together."

After dinner, dishwashing, and some TV, Grace and Giselle headed off to bed while Rollie and Gloria took Buddy around the block.

Rollie showed Gloria how you could tell Buddy was a good dog, because he didn't pull or try to yank away like most pups do.

Rollie had bought a roll of poop bags, and Gloria had several in her pocket.

"Can we get Buddy boots and a jacket for the winter?" Gloria said.

"I was thinking we could all refresh our winter coats and boots."

"I know me and Giselle are pretty sick of hand-me-downs."

"When I grew up, I had hand-me-downs of hand-me-downs, but I understand. We'll pick a date next week."

Back home, Gloria changed and went to bed.

Rollie went to his office, opened the little wooden box, and checked his equipment. He charged the batteries and then left the box on his desk and locked the office.

Before going to bed, Rollie peeked into Gloria's bedroom.

She was asleep, under just a sheet, with Buddy curled up beside her.

Rollie went to bed, but his mind was preoccupied with Knox, and sleep was far off in the distance.

Knox had confided with his lawyers and they came up with a strategy of some kind. Offense or defense, which?

Without ever quite falling asleep, Rollie woke up at 3:00 a.m. when he heard a noise in the kitchen. He went to investigate.

Gloria was at the sliding door.

"Everything okay?" Rollie said.

"Small dog, tiny bladder," Gloria said.

Rollie filled two glasses with milk. "Want a cookie?" he said.

CHAPTER FORTY-ONE

Rollie wore a suit and tie for the meeting with Knox.

In Teal's office, Rollie set his portable tape recorder and the small wooden box on Teal's desk.

"The tie pin is a transmitter," Rollie said. "The ear piece is the receiver."

Teal picked up the ear piece. "And the recorder is for?"

"Hold the ear piece to the microphone," Rollie said. "You'll hear every word while it's recording."

"Let's give it a test," Teal said.

Rollie put the tie pin on his tie. "Turn the recorder on while I step outside," he said.

In the hallway, Rollie said, "What would you like for lunch, Bill?"

The door opened and Teal said, "A thick, juicy steak."

•   •   •

"Wait until I get inside to turn on the recorder or the first sixty seconds will be nothing but street traffic," Rollie said.

"I should be in there with you," Teal said.

"It's better that you do the recording for evidence," Rollie said. "I'll be alright inside, and you can watch the street."

Rollie left Teal's unmarked car, crossed the street, and entered

Knox's headquarters. A crowd of about three hundred people were inside, with at least one hundred manning the phones.

A woman approached Rollie. "May I help you, sir?"

Karl stepped out of the crowd. "It's okay, Cheryl, he's with me."

Rollie looked at Karl and Karl grinned. "This way," he said.

Rollie followed Karl to the office, and the moment Rollie was inside, Karl said, "I get to frisk you."

Rollie held up his arms while Karl patted him down.

"Where's Knox?" Rollie said.

"He'll be right in. I just want you to know that before this is over, I'm going to pay you back for the kick in the balls."

"No need," Rollie said. "It was my pleasure."

A side door opened. Knox walked in, went to his desk, and sat in his chair.

"He's clean," Karl said.

"Karl, would you wait outside, please," Knox said.

Rollie walked to a chair opposite the desk and sat down. "This is your party, Mr. Knox, why don't you tell me why you invited me?"

"Like I said on the phone, some friendly talk."

"My friends don't usually pat me down," Rollie said.

"Karl used to be a cop. All cops are a bit paranoid."

Knox coupled his hands and looked at Rollie.

"As lieutenant governor, I can do only so much to help the people of New York," Knox said. "But as governor, that is where I can really accomplish so much for this state and its citizens."

"If you're stumping for my vote, you don't have it," Rollie said.

Knox grinned his boyish grin. "I didn't think I did," he said. "So, let's get down to brass tacks. If the police had anything on me, as you claim, they would have arrested me by now. My lawyers have investigated the three pearl necklaces left unclaimed on the victim's website, and there is no evidence that any of them belonged to my wife, so your trick is pointless."

"I'm not so sure about that," Rollie said. "It may be true at this point the police have no just cause to arrest you, but as you well know, there are no limitations on murder. So, who knows what the future holds?"

"May I ask why you believe so strongly that I murdered Julia?" Knox said.

"It's simple," Rollie said. "The phone call with her sister. She couldn't have made it to Tower One in time for the plane to hit. All the other little things, like your speeding ticket a week later, the pearls, the fact that you sold your cabin in the mountains… they may not add up to much, but that phone call will be your downfall, Knox."

"And yet, here I sit without any fear of the police or you," Knox said. "Why is that, do you suppose?"

"My guess is you're overconfident," Rollie said. "Or just plain stupid."

Knox grinned and then laughed. "You got balls, Finch, I'll give you that," he said. "You must be a hell of a card player. Go ahead and have me arrested, see where it gets you."

"Who said I wanted you arrested?" Rollie said.

"Then what the fuck do you want?" Knox said.

"Doubt," Rollie said.

"What?" Knox said. "Doubt?"

"In the eyes of the voters," Rollie said. "Which will happen when I make this entire mess public. And as much as the *Times* and the cable shows may be on your side, they are in the business of ratings and selling papers, and they will cover it and then you will lose the election."

"I don't think so," Knox said.

"You're wrong about me being a card player," Rollie said. "I am, however a hell of a chess player. Do you know the secret to chess, Mr. Knox?"

"I'm afraid I don't play," Knox said.

"The secret to playing chess is patience, that's all."

"My lawyers will be in touch, Mr. Finch," Knox said.

"Of course they will," Rollie said.

Rollie stood up and walked to the door.

"See you soon," Knox said, "Mr. Finch."

Rollie walked out through the busy headquarters, past the crowd and to the street. "Bill, pick me up on 53rd. Let me know if Lurch follows me."

Rollie walked to the corner and crossed over to 52nd. At 53rd, he waited by the curb for Teal to pick him up.

Rollie opened the car door and got in beside Teal.

"Followed you the whole way," Teal said.

"Let's get some lunch," Rollie said.

$$\bullet \ \bullet \ \bullet$$

Rollie chose the Pub and Brew on West 73rd and Eighth.

"This burger is enormous," Teal said. "And these fries are the size of pickles."

"You heard it all, what do you think?" Rollie said.

"Knox is one suave bastard, I'll give him that," Teal said. "I heard anger in his voice several times, but he never caved."

"Did you ever hear him deny he killed his wife?" Rollie said.

"Not directly, no."

"I guess I'll wait to hear from his lawyers," Rollie said.

"Can you burn off a copy of that tape for me?" Teal said.

Rollie nodded. "Want dessert?"

"Do birds fly?" Teal said.

"Not if they're overweight," Rollie said.

CHAPTER FORTY-TWO

Rollie listened to the tape several times before burning off two copies.

Then he played it at least a dozen more times so he could write down every word spoken by him and Knox.

He then typed up the conversation on his computer and saved it as a document.

While the girls prepared dinner, Rollie called Joanna and told her about the Knox meeting.

"It sounds like he might be a bit worried," Joanna said.

"More than a bit if he's coming after me with his lawyers," Rollie said.

"Rollie, I know I haven't paid you enough for…" Joanna said.

"I'm working for myself now," Rollie said, "so don't worry about bills or payments."

"What will you do about his lawyers?" Joanna said.

"When they call, I'll talk to them." Rollie said.

"Please be careful, Rollie," Joanna said. "Knox is a snake."

"The best way to kill a snake is to cut off the head," Rollie said. "I'll call you soon."

Rollie went to see what the girls were doing in the kitchen. A large Crockpot was on the counter and the kitchen smelled of fresh bread.

"Mom's recipe for beef stew and homemade Italian bread," Grace said.

"Where's Buddy?" Rollie said.

"In the backyard," Gloria said.

"How long does that stew need?" Rollie said.

"Another thirty minutes," Grace said.

Rollie grabbed a can of ginger ale, went to the backyard and sat at the patio table. Buddy was lying down in the shade beside the fence and he looked at Rollie.

"Come here, boy," Rollie said.

Buddy got up and jogged over to Rollie and sniffed his hand.

"Do you like your new home?" Rollie said. "The girls treating you well?"

Buddy responded by jumping onto Rollie's lap, and Rollie scratched him behind the ears.

"This doesn't mean you can sleep in my bed," Rollie said.

Gloria appeared with Buddy's leash. "Feel like a walk around the block, Dad?" she said.

"Sure," Rollie said.

Gloria attached the leash and they went out through the gate in the fence.

"Dad, school starts in ten days," Gloria said.

"Your last year before high school," Rollie said.

"That's not what I mean," Gloria said. "With me gone from 7:30 until 3:30, Buddy will need to be walked."

"Well, I changed your diaper, I suppose I can do the same for Buddy," Rollie said.

"What about when you're working?" Gloria said.

"I have an idea about that," Rollie said.

"What?"

"You'll see."

After walking completely around the block, Rollie led Gloria and Buddy to their next door neighbor's house.

"Mrs. Kravitz?" Gloria said.

"How many times have I shoveled her walk and driveway?" Rollie said. "I'll stop by there tonight, and I'm sure she'll be fine with it."

When they returned home, Grace and Giselle were setting the table. "Dinner's ready," Grace said.

At the table, Rollie said, "It's come to my attention that you three need new winter boots," Rollie said.

"I can get by," Gloria said. "I have Grace's old…"

"Grace, do you think you can safely transport your sisters to the mall tomorrow to buy each of you new winter boots?" Rollie said.

"Yes, of course," Grace said.

"After dinner, go online and see what you want, and let me know the cost," Rollie said.

"We can do that," Grace said.

•　　•　　•

In his office, Rollie sent a copy of the transcript of the recorded Knox conversation to Teal's office computer.

Then he read it one more time, looking for anything he might possibly use against Knox's lawyers.

The girls knocked on the door and filed in.

"We shopped like you said, and the average price is one seventy-nine a pair," Grace said.

"Go get them in the morning," Rollie said. "Buddy can stay home with me."

"Thanks, Dad," Grace said.

"And Grace, think of the cargo you're hauling," Rollie said.

"I know, and I will," Grace said.

After the girls left, Rollie checked the tie pin and receiver. Both were good for one city block, more than enough to record the conversation with Knox's lawyers when the time came.

He didn't want to involve Teal again, so he needed a way to plant the receiver and recorder in range.

"The men's room," Rollie said aloud.

CHAPTER FORTY-THREE

After breakfast, Rollie gave Grace eight hundred dollars that she put into the money belt she wore under her loose-fitting blouse.

"Call me when you get to the mall and again when you leave," Rollie said.

"What's the extra money for?" Grace said.

"Tax, gas, tolls, and lunch," Rollie said. "I'll take care of dinner."

After the girl's left, Rollie took a mug of coffee and went into the backyard with Buddy. He sat at the patio table while Buddy ran around chasing birds, insects, and butterflies.

The call on Rollie's cell phone came at 11:15.

"Mr. Finch, this is Peters and Schram, attorneys for Mr. John Knox," the voice said.

"I'm familiar with your firm," Rollie said. "And I've been expecting your call."

"Would you be willing to have a conversation with us tomorrow morning, say, eleven o'clock?"

"I don't see why not," Rollie said.

"If you're familiar with our firm then I assume you'll know where to find us. Until tomorrow," the voice said.

Rollie called Teal at his office.

"I just got a call from Knox's lawyers, Peters and Schram," Rollie said. "Know them?"

"They're the princes of fucking darkness when it comes to defense attorneys," Teal said. "Seven figure guys all the way."

"Tomorrow should be interesting," Rollie said.

"Want moral support?"

"I'll fly solo on this one," Rollie said. "We don't want them accusing us of police harassment."

"So, you should be done around lunchtime," Teal said.

Grace was calling in just then.

"Bill, I gotta go; Grace is on the other line. I'll swing by tomorrow after the sit-down."

"We're at the mall," Grace said when Rollie switched over to her call. "We'll leave in about an hour and be home soon."

"Okay, and tell Gloria I'll be taking Buddy for a walk," Rollie said.

"Okay, Dad."

Rollie put his cell phone in his pocket, leashed Buddy and took him out through the gate in the fence.

They walked around the block, which gave Buddy ample time to sniff and explore, and do his business.

When they returned home, Rollie took a mug of coffee to the office and gave Buddy the run of the house.

Rollie went through his files and pulled out a case file for Peters and Schram. Sixteen months ago, Rollie was hired to do some background work for a case being handled by a junior partner. He never met Peters or Schram, but he did visit their suite of offices several times.

If you couldn't write a seven figure retainer, they weren't your lawyers. They also had a standard relationship with the Catholic Church, so Peters and Schram were anything but poor.

What they were, to paraphrase Teal, were the princes of fucking darkness.

CHAPTER FORTY-FOUR

Rollie parked on 31st and Park Avenue South and walked to the offices of Peters and Schram on 34th. They were on the twenty-first floor of an all-glass high rise.

He arrived ten minutes early. "I have an eleven o'clock appointment with Mr. Peters and Schram, but I wonder if I may use the restroom first?" Rollie said to the receptionist.

"Certainly," she said. "Down the hall on the right."

Rollie followed the hallway to the men's room and entered. It was large, bright and airy, with a long countertop and two sinks.

Earlier, Rollie had taped the receiver to the built-in microphone on the mini recorder and he used duct tape from a small roll to tape it under the counter.

"Be back for you later," he said.

Rollie returned to the receptionist, who escorted him to a conference room where Peters and Schram were waiting.

"Mr. Finch, please have a seat," Peters said. "Would you like some coffee?"

"I would," Rollie said as he took a chair.

Schram filled three porcelain cups from a silver coffee pot and then sat beside Peters.

Both men appeared to be in their sixties. Both wore impeccable suits and had perfect, pricey haircuts.

"Shall we begin?" Peters said with a practiced smile.

"I'm all ears," Rollie said.

"We represent Mr. John Knox as you're aware, and frankly, your harassment of our client has to stop, and it stops today," Peters said.

"Or what?" Rollie said.

"Excuse me?" Peters said.

"You said my harassment of your client must stop at once," Rollie said. "Or else, what happens?"

"I'm afraid a court order will follow," Schram said.

"Is that all?" Rollie said.

"I'm afraid you're not taking this seriously, Mr. Finch," Schram said.

"You guys are afraid a lot," Rollie said.

"Why did I have the feeling you would be uncooperative?" Peters said.

"Probably because Knox told you I would be," Rollie said.

"We're prepared to sue you for harassment of our client," Schram said. "We've checked you out thoroughly, Mr. Finch, and I promise you that you will lose your license and you'll have to sell your home to pay your legal fees."

"I guess you didn't check me out thoroughly enough," Rollie said. "See, you guys hired me a year ago to do some criminal work. People v. Stevens. I testified in court on your behalf. I believe your client was acquitted."

"What?" Peters said.

"You're going to look pretty stupid in the media once word gets out about that, don't you think? You suddenly saying that the consultant you hired is a problem," Rollie said. "Those million dollar clients of yours don't pay you to look foolish in public, do they?"

"Wait. Let's talk about this," Schram said.

"Your client murdered his wife, and I aim to prove it," Rollie said. "So unless you want your firm to look very foolish on the cable news shows and the front page of the *Times*, get out of my way."

Rollie stood, walked to the door, looked back and said, "Thanks for the coffee."

He returned to the bathroom, retrieved the mini-recorder, and left the office of Peters and Schram.

•   •   •

"Jesus Fucking Christ, these guys are stupid," Teal said after he listened to the tape.

"I caught a lucky break," Rollie said.

"Is it enough for them to back off?" Teal said.

"They will mull it around for a few days, weigh their options, and realize future business depends on their reputation," Rollie said. "If word gets out they were too lazy to check the man they once hired before they threatened him: sloppy work doesn't get million dollar retainers. They will back off."

"Leaving Knox where?" Teal said.

"Very pissed off," Rollie said.

"Let's go to lunch," Teal said.

•   •   •

At the diner a few blocks away, Teal ordered a large bowl of chili, a bacon cheeseburger with fries, and a large glass of milk.

"The milk neutralizes the chili," Teal said.

Rollie ordered a chicken sandwich with fries and ginger ale.

"You never really answered my question about what you think Knox is going to do next," Teal said.

"I guess that's going to depend on how badly he wants to be governor," Rollie said.

Teal ate some chili and washed it down with milk.

"And I expect we'll know the answer to that soon enough," Rollie said.

"Burn off a copy of the new tape for me," Teal said. "Andrews loved the first one."

Rollie nodded.

Teal ate more chili.

CHAPTER FORTY-FIVE

Rollie was burning off copies of the taped conversation with Peters and Schram when he heard the girls carrying on in the house.

He went to investigate.

In the living room, Grace was wearing her prom dress and shoes while Giselle and Gloria stood around her and examined her look.

"I'll never get it right, never," Grace said.

"What's going on in here?" Rollie said.

"It's her hair, Dad," Giselle said.

"What's wrong with her hair?" Rollie said.

"The welcome back to school dance is tomorrow night, Dad," Grace said. "And my hair is a mess."

"It's not prom-y enough," Gloria said.

"Oh for... well, go get it done, then," Rollie said.

"Dad, a prom wash, cut and style is, like, a hundred dollars," Grace said.

"Call that place, make an appointment for tomorrow afternoon, and get it done," Rollie said. "And you can pay me back by making dinner tonight."

"Come on, girls, help me change," Grace said, and the girls rushed off to her bedroom.

"And there's still two more of them," Rollie said to himself.

He returned to the office and finished burning off copies of the tape. Then he did an hour on the step climber.

• • •

All showered and changed from the workout, Rollie started creating a transcript of the conversation with Peters and Schram. Buddy lay at the corner of his desk, whining a bit. "Do you have to go out?" Rollie asked.

He went to the kitchen, but the girls were still in Grace's room. He grabbed the leash off the counter and took Buddy for a walk.

On the sidewalk, Rollie turned to the right and took Buddy around the block. Halfway home, Rollie's cop's sixth sense tingled on the back of his neck and he began to scan the block.

Same houses, lawns, and people.

So why the tingle?

When he reached home, Rollie scanned the street carefully. Nothing looked out of the ordinary.

And yet?

Rollie took Buddy inside where Buddy rushed to Gloria in the kitchen. The girls were starting dinner.

"Dad, I made the appointment for two o'clock tomorrow," Grace said.

"Okay," Rollie said. "Call me when dinner is ready."

He returned to the office and opened the garage door and walked out to the front lawn. Across the street, a neighbor was mowing his lawn. A couple passed by walking their dog.

Rollie looked to his left and then to his right and the tingling sensation on the back of his neck started again.

Then he saw it, what he had missed earlier.

The red flag on the mailbox was raised. He only raised the flag when he put outgoing mail in that he wanted the carrier to pick up.

Rollie walked across his lawn and opened the mailbox. A single bullet was inside. He returned to the office for a cloth and a plastic evidence bag, then went back to the mailbox and retrieved the bullet.

Back in the office, he called Teal.

"Bill, feel like having dinner at my house tonight?" Rollie said.

"What are you having?"

"Does it matter? Anything is better than plain lettuce and carrot sticks."

"And what do I tell the wife?"

"You have an emergency."

"And do I?"

"You'll see in about an hour," Rollie said.

After hanging up, Rollie went to the kitchen.

"Girls, your Uncle Bill is coming to dinner. Did you make enough?" Rollie said.

"To feed a small army," Grace said.

. . .

"There's some lasagna left, Uncle Bill," Grace said.

"And one piece of garlic bread," Giselle said.

Teal looked at Rollie. "Rollie?"

"I'm stuffed," Rollie said.

"In that case…" Teal said.

After finishing off the lasagna and garlic bread, Rollie took Teal to the office and closed the door.

"And the emergency is?" Teal said.

Rollie opened a desk drawer and handed Teal the plastic evidence bag with the bullet in it. "In my mailbox this afternoon," Rollie said.

Teal took the envelope and looked at the bullet. ".40 caliber, probably a Glock," he said.

"It's probably clean, but have it dusted anyway," Rollie said.

"Knox didn't waste any time sending a message, did he?" Teal said.

"Check Clapper's gun permit, see what firearms he owns," Rollie said.

"Lurch?"

"The same."

"Want a car to sweep by every couple of hours?" Teal said.

"Knox won't go that far," Rollie said. "This was just meant to excite me."

"And did it?"

"You know better than that."

"I'll call you tomorrow after I check Clapper's permit," Teal said.

Rollie reached into his desk for a pack of breath mints and handed it to Teal. "So you don't smell like lasagna and garlic rolls," he said.

CHAPTER FORTY-SIX

Rollie was in his office after an hour on the step climber when Teal called.

"Rollie, it's Bill," Teal said. "The bullet is clean, but Clapper has a permit and owns a Glock 24 and a 26, both chambered in .40 caliber."

"No surprise," Rollie said.

"I'm not liking this, Rollie," Teal said.

"It's just bluster," Rollie said. "Knox is letting me know he's done his homework on me, that's all. His lawyers let him down, so he's beating his chest."

"I'd feel better if you let me have a car swing by every few hours," Teal said. "Those three daughters of yours are precious cargo and damn fine cooks."

"Okay, but only after dark," Rollie said. "I don't want the girls getting spooked."

"You got it," Teal said.

After hanging up with Teal, Rollie heard the girls arrive home from the hair salon.

He met them in the living room.

"What do you think, Dad?" Grace said.

Grace's hair was worn in an elegant bun with a sweep of bangs. "Very nice," he said.

"Come on girls, help me get dressed," Grace said.

"What time is the dance?" Rollie said.

"7:00," Grace said.

"It's four o'clock in the afternoon," Rollie said.

"I'll need at least two hours to get dressed," Grace said. "Come on girls."

After the girls went to Grace's room, Rollie grabbed a can of ginger ale and returned to his office.

"And this, times three," he said.

He was reading the transcript he'd made of the Peters and Schram conversation when Knox called on his cell phone.

Doing a Bogart impersonation, Knox said, "Of all the law firms in the world, you have to walk into mine."

"You invited me," Rollie said. "You should know never to invite the vampire in."

"It's a small world, who knew?" Knox said.

"Not that small," Rollie said. "What do you want?"

"I thought we could meet and work this out, come to some sort of resolution," Knox said.

"You mean like the bullet left in my mailbox?" Rollie said.

"I don't know what you're talking about," Knox said.

"Ask Karl," Rollie said.

"I told him to do no such thing," Knox said.

"That doesn't mean he didn't do it," Rollie said. "It's a .40 caliber bullet, and Karl owns two Glocks, both .40 caliber."

"I'm running for governor, for God's sake," Knox said. "I wouldn't authorize Karl to do something like that."

"That still doesn't mean he didn't do it," Rollie said.

"I'm in Manhattan on Monday, can we please meet and talk?" Knox said. "Maybe we can find some common ground."

"Where and when?" Rollie said.

"My headquarters around 1:00 in the afternoon," Knox said. "I'll be free the rest of the day, and we can have a long talk."

"I'll see you at 1:00," Rollie said.

"One thing before I go, I really didn't have anything to do with that bullet," Knox said.

"See you at 1:00," Rollie said.

Rollie hung up and called Teal at home. "Feel like riding shotgun again on Monday?" he said.

"Knox?"

"Monday at one o'clock. He denies knowing about the bullet."

"Of course he does," Teal said. "Let's try that muffin burger place on 48th and Eighth Avenue."

"You buying?" Rollie said.

"Don't be ridiculous," Teal said. "My wife has me on an allowance."

"I'll pick you up at noon," Rollie said.

"Rollie, it looks like you got to him," Teal said.

"Yeah," Rollie said.

He made an entry into the file about Knox's phone call, then checked the mini-recorder and tie pin transmitter.

About to call it quits for the day, Giselle opened the office door. "Dad, Grace wants you to take a look," she said.

Rollie went to the living room with Giselle.

Grace, her hair, makeup, gown, and shoes ready, looked as beautiful as her mother when Rollie first met her.

"Well?" Grace said.

"Your mother would approve," Rollie said.

"Thanks, Dad," Grace said. "When James gets here, I'll be in my room. Talk to him for a bit so I can make an entrance."

"Make an…?" Rollie said.

"Come on, girls," Grace said and they dashed off to Grace's room.

"One of you couldn't be a boy?" Rollie sighed.

At six o'clock, James Seymour arrived, corsage in hand.

"Hello, Mr. Finch, I'm here to take Grace to the dance," James said.

"You don't say," Rollie said.

"Yes sir, don't you remember?" James said.

"James, you're wearing a blue tux and carrying a corsage, I didn't think you were here to sweep my front steps," Rollie said.

"No, sir," James said. "I mean, I will if you want me to, but I'm here for the dance."

"James, come to my office for a moment," Rollie said.

Rollie led James to the office.

"Have you a car?" Rollie said.

"A car? No sir," James said.

"A license?" Rollie said.

"Yes sir."

"Do you think you can drive my Buick?" Rollie said.

"My Dad has a Buick like yours and I drive it all the time," James said.

"Well, you can't take the subway to the dance, and you'd feel pretty foolish if Grace drove you in her car, so I'll lend you my Buick for the evening," Rollie said.

"Thank you, Mr. Finch," James said.

"Here are the rules," Rollie said. "I know it's less than a mile to school, but no speeding and you drive carefully. Most accidents happen within one mile of home. And when you escort Grace to the car, you open the door for her first. Got that?"

"Yes sir," James said. "Sir, may I ask a question?"

"Go ahead."

"Where does the corsage go? On the girl, I mean."

"You place it on Grace's left wrist."

"Left wrist, got it."

"Here are the car keys," Rollie said. "Now let's wait for Grace in the living room."

Grace made her fashionably late appearance in the living room at 6:30.

"James will be taking my car," Rollie said.

"Thanks, Dad," Grace said.

"I got this for you," James said. "It goes on the left wrist."

After James placed the corsage on Grace's left wrist, he escorted her from the house to the car.

Giselle and Gloria watched from the window.

"He opened the door for her," Gloria said.

"I want a boyfriend," Giselle said.

"And I want some dinner," Rollie said. "Gloria, grab Buddy and let's go get some takeout."

Rollie took Grace's car to the strip mall on Queens Boulevard where they ordered Chinese takeout.

Gloria and Giselle took Buddy for a walk around the parking lot while Rollie went into the restaurant to pick up the food.

On the way back to the car, Rollie spotted Karl standing at the edge of the parking lot, watching Giselle and Gloria.

Rollie walked toward Karl and Karl jumped into a black SUV and quickly drove away.

"Girls, let's go," Rollie said.

•   •   •

James and Grace showed up at exactly eleven o'clock, and she, Giselle, and Grace went off to her room.

Before going to bed, Rollie went to his office, opened the door to the street and looked around for signs of Karl.

Around midnight, he finally went to bed.

CHAPTER FORTY-SEVEN

When Rollie entered Knox's headquarters on Monday at 1:00 in the afternoon, Karl approached him.

"If you follow my daughters again, I will kill you and happily go to jail," Rollie said

Karl grinned. "I don't know what you're talking about," he said.

"Keep following me and you'll find out," Rollie said.

"The boss wants to…" Karl said.

Rollie walked past Karl to Knox's office, opened the door and stepped inside.

Knox, ever-perfect suit and hair, was behind his desk.

"Please come in and have a seat," Knox said.

Rollie took a chair opposite the desk.

"Last night, my daughter went to her welcome back to school prom," Rollie said. "I took my other two daughters out for Chinese food, and who did I see in the parking lot but Karl Clapper. Now what is Clapper doing in a parking lot in Queens where I just so happened to be with my daughters?"

"I didn't know that," Knox said.

"He works for you, doesn't he?" Rollie said.

"And I'll speak to him," Knox said.

"Like you did after the bullet?" Rollie said.

Knox sighed. "This has gone too far," he said. "Look, Finch, I'm up ten to twelve points in the polls—do you really think I would resort to something like that at this point?"

"You said you wanted to talk to me, so talk," Rollie said.

"What will it take to get you to stop this vendetta against me?" Knox said.

"A confession, for starters," Rollie said.

"To what? I haven't done anything," Knox said.

"Besides murder your wife, you mean," Rollie said.

"I underestimated you, Finch," Knox said. "Peters and Schram told me that same thing after your meeting with them. I won't make that mistake again."

"You're talking but you're not saying much," Rollie said.

"Will you back off?" Knox said.

"No," Rollie said. "In fact, I'm prepared to dump this entire mess in the laps of the FBI and the *New York Times*."

Knox stared at Rollie for several seconds. "I wouldn't do that," he said.

"No? Why not?" Rollie said.

"Do you know what they used to say about England when it ruled the world?" Knox said.

"England makes a great ally but a bad enemy," Rollie said.

"You don't want me for an enemy, Finch," Knox said.

"If you're going to hire a new attorney, keep in mind that in the last four years, I've done work for about forty of them," Rollie said. "You might want to do your homework next time."

"I tried," Knox said. "Lord knows I tried."

"I guess we're done then," Rollie said.

"For now," Knox said.

Rollie stood, walked to the door, opened it and stepped out to the very busy headquarters center.

He walked past Karl, who said, "Hey, Finch, I want to..." and out to the street where Teal was waiting in his car.

•   •   •

As Teal bit into a juicy bacon muffin burger, he said, "Novel idea serving burgers on English muffins."

"You heard the entire conversation, what do you think?" Rollie said.

"I think he's fuming mad and will retaliate," Teal said.

"That's what I think," Rollie said. "But how?"

"This is what we police call a wait-and-see moment," Teal said. "However, I will call in a few favors and make sure a car sweeps your block every hour after dark until further notice."

"Knox is too smart to try something at home," Rollie said.

"His clown is not," Teal said. "And I'd feel better about it."

"Okay, do it," Rollie said.

Teal flagged a waitress. "Let me get another of these," he said.

"After I burn off a copy for you, get it over to Andrews," Rollie said. "See if he wants a meeting."

Teal nodded as he finished off his burger. "Soon as I get back to the office, I'll give him a call."

"Then call me later at home," Rollie said.

•   •   •

When Rollie walked through his front door, the girls were in the living room.

"We made something for you, Dad," Grace said. "Go change out of the suit and we'll show you."

Rollie went to his bedroom and changed into comfortable sweats and returned to the living room.

"Have a seat," Grace said as she removed a DVD disc from a wrapper.

"We spent two weeks going through a lot of old family films and put this together for you," Giselle said.

"We saved some of our new boots money to have it done professionally at the mall," Gloria said.

Grace put the disc into the DVD player and hit the play button.

The words 'For Mom' appeared on the TV. Followed by the word 'Us and Mom.'

Then a collage of film clips taken from films Rollie took over the years followed. The highlight was Georgia swimming with a dolphin in a side-by-side shot of each of the girls swimming with a dolphin in the same lagoon.

The ending had Rollie choked up a bit. It was a side-by-side film of Georgia smiling at Rollie with the Key West sunset behind her and of the girls in the same place, smiling at him with the sunset at their backs.

"Girls, I don't know what to say," Rollie said. "I think I'll take Buddy for a walk."

Rollie leashed up Buddy and took him for a walk around the block. The neighborhood was quiet. A few people were mowing their lawns; a couple was walking their dog, a few people waved to Rollie as he led Buddy on the leash.

When he reached home, the girls were waiting for him in the living room.

"We have another surprise for you, Dad," Grace said.

"Remember all the shopping trips we did this summer?" Gloria said. "Well, we looked for stuff on sale so we wouldn't spend it all, and we saved quite a bit of money."

"And we're using it to take you to dinner tonight," Gloria said.

"We made reservations for 6:30 at The Roma," Grace said.

"We'll take my car."

"Be ready by 6:15," Giselle said.

"Okay, I will," Rollie said.

Rollie went to his office and called Teal.

"Bill, I think I'm turning everything over to the FBI," Rollie said. "You're right about one thing, my girls are priceless."

"When?" Teal said.

"I'll call the regional FBI office tomorrow morning and make an appointment," Rollie said.

"It's the smart move, Rollie," Teal said.

"Let me call Andrews," Rollie said.

"Sure."

After hanging up with Teal, Rollie did an hour on the step climber and then took a shower and changed.

At 6:15, Rollie met the girls in the living room.

"So, Dad, seeing as how we're paying for dinner, can I have a boyfriend now?" Giselle said.

"No," Rollie said.

CHAPTER FORTY-EIGHT

Before calling the FBI regional office in Manhattan, Rollie called Joanna first. She didn't answer her cell phone, so he tried the hard line and again she didn't answer.

He gave it a few minutes and called back, leaving messages on both lines.

Maybe she was teaching? Rollie knew school started earlier down south, but he wasn't sure exactly when.

He decided to wait on the call to the FBI until after he reached Joanna.

He changed into sweats and did an hour on the step climber. Then he called Joanna's hard line and cell phone again without success.

After a shower and change of clothes, Rollie grabbed a mug of coffee and returned to the office. Joanna still hadn't called.

He searched through the stored numbers for Joanna's mother in Florida and punched in the number. It rang six times before the call was transferred to voice mail.

Rollie hung up without leaving a message.

Something was wrong; he could sense it, just as he had sensed the bullet in the mailbox.

He called Teal at his office.

"Bill, I'm going to hold off on the FBI for a bit," he said.

"Because?" Teal said.

"I've been trying to call Joanna all morning and she doesn't answer her hard line or cell," Rollie said. "I even tried her mother in Florida."

"Maybe they took a vacation?"

"Joanna is a school teacher and I think school already started down there," Rollie said.

"Maybe she's in school, then?"

"Let me check," Rollie said. "I'll call you back."

Rollie hung up and pulled the 'for hire' paperwork on Joanna. The school where she taught was listed with a phone number.

He called the school and asked for the administrator. The administrator said Joanna called out for the day.

Rollie called Teal again. "She called out from school," he said.

"Before you go thinking the worst, let me contact the local PD and have them check her house," Teal said.

"Her mother's, too," Rollie said.

"Give me the addresses," Teal said.

Rollie read off the addresses and then said, "Call me on my cell."

·　　·　　·

Rollie took his car to the dog park, even though it was just a six-block walk. He parked on the street, entered the park, waved to the girls, and took a seat on the bench.

Karl came up behind the bench and sat beside Rollie.

"Don't react," Karl said. "Stay nice and calm. The boss wants to talk to you."

Karl handed Rollie a cell phone.

"Knox," Rollie said.

"I'm sorry it had to come to this, Finch," Knox said. "I tried to reason with you, but you just wouldn't listen."

"What do you want?" Rollie said.

"I'll tell you what I *don't* want and that is to hurt those three beautiful daughters of yours," Knox said. "I've been watching them on Karl's cell phone, and they are just lovely. You must be very proud of them."

"Stay the hell away from my daughters," Rollie said.

"What happens next depends on you," Knox said.

"What happened to Joanna Kearns?" Rollie said.

"She took her mother on a Caribbean cruise at my request," Knox said.

"What do you want, Knox?" Rollie said.

"You are to stop your investigation of me immediately," Knox said. "If not, Karl gets to do what Karl does best. Understood?"

"Yes."

"I want all paperwork and documents pertaining to me no later than ten o'clock tonight," Knox said. "Karl will pick them up at your house. Understood?"

"Yes."

"And I mean every scrap of paper you have on me," Knox said. "And then you tell the police you've given up on me because there isn't any evidence to proceed on. Understood?"

"Yes."

"Ever see a pack of wolves?" Knox said. "They growl and show teeth in a display of bravado, but then they all meekly submit to the alpha. You're part of the pack, and I'm the alpha. It's just the way it is, Finch."

"There will be no trouble from me," Rollie said.

"Then Karl will see you at 10:00 tonight," Knox said and hung up.

Rollie returned the phone to Karl.

"Any tricks tonight and I'll kill them right in front of you," Karl said. "Am I clear?"

"Yes."

"Knox hates surprises and so do I. Keep that in mind," Karl said. "If I even smell a cop within ten square blocks, I won't show. I'll return another day when you don't expect it and I'll take it out on them."

Karl nodded to the girls.

"My girls mean more to me than Knox," Rollie said.

"Good. See you at ten o'clock," Karl said.

"Come in through the garage," Rollie said. "That's where my office is."

Karl nodded, stood up, and left the dog park.

Rollie took out his cell phone and called Teal.

"Never mind, I found Joanna Kearns," Rollie said. "She took her mother on a cruise."

"That's a relief," Teal said.

"I'll still hold off on contacting the FBI until she returns, out of courtesy to her as my client," Rollie said.

"A few days won't hurt anything," Teal said.

"No it won't," Rollie said. "Right now, I'm taking the girls for ice cream."

"Have a scoop for me," Teal said.

Rollie stood up, pocketed the phone and walked to the girls. "Buddy looks hot; let's take him for ice cream."

•   •   •

Before dinner, Rollie went to his office and made copies of everything pertaining to Knox, put the copies into a large manila enveloped, addressed it to Teal's home address, and used his postal scale to get the correct postage.

He told the girls he would be right back, drove to the post

office, and dropped the envelope into a mailbox.

Later at dinner, Rollie told the girls he had a new client coming tonight at 10:00 and asked them to be in bed by 9:30.

"We're tired anyway, Dad," Grace said.

"Good," Rollie said "I'll tackle the dishes."

After some TV, the girls headed off to bed at 9:30.

Rollie locked the front and back door, left just nightlights on, and went to his office.

He opened the garage door and then sat behind the desk to wait.

CHAPTER FORTY-NINE

Time drew out like a long blade as Rollie sat and waited for Karl to appear.

Finally, at one minute past 10:00, Karl strolled into the office from the street.

He was smoking a cigarette, and tossed it to the floor and stepped on it.

"Let's get to it," Karl said.

"All my documents are in my safe," Rollie said.

"Open it," Karl said.

Rollie stood and walked to the back wall and opened the converted tool chest. Karl followed closely behind. Rollie removed a tall stack of documents and handed them over.

Karl looked at the empty top shelf. "Now the file cabinet and desk drawers."

Rollie went to the desk and allowed Karl to rifle through every drawer.

"The file cabinet," Karl said.

"Help yourself," Rollie said. "It's not locked."

Karl set the documents on the desk and then went through the four drawers of the file cabinet.

"Satisfied?" Rollie said.

"Not quite," Karl said. "Your computer."

Rollie sat behind the desk. "What do you want to see?" he said.

"You deleting everything with Knox's name on it," Karl said.

Rollie opened his case file and all the documents popped up by date.

"Delete them permanently," Karl said.

Rollie deleted the files and then cleared all deleted files permanently from the hard drive.

"That's it, that's everything," Rollie said.

"Stand up," Karl said.

Rollie said.

"If we ever hear from you again, think about those girls of yours," Karl said.

Rollie nodded.

Karl made a fist of his right hand and drove a punch deep into Rollie's stomach with all of his two hundred and fifty pounds behind it.

Rollie saw the punch coming and tightened his abdomen, but the punch had so much force behind it that it knocked Rollie to the floor and left him breathless.

"That's for the kick in the balls," Karl said.

Karl grabbed the stack of documents, turned and walked out of the garage.

Rollie stayed on the floor for several minutes until he was able to regain some air in his lungs and then stood up very slowly.

For a few seconds, he felt dizzy and thought he might pass out, but he held on, took some deep breaths, and his head cleared. He closed the garage door and locked it, and then went to his bedroom and took a hot shower to clear his mind.

He toweled dry and looked at the red bruise on his stomach in the mirror. Then he tossed on pajamas and went to check on the girls. They always slept with their doors open and a nightlight on.

Grace, always a hot sleeper, had tossed the covers away.

Giselle, the opposite, was wrapped up like a cocoon.

Gloria had her right arm draped over Buddy as they snuggled together.

Rollie went to the kitchen for a glass of milk. He thought about what had just happened. The lives of his three daughters had been threatened.

That was not acceptable.

And neither was murder.

CHAPTER FIFTY

Rollie checked his notebook for the owner of the property on Big Pond Lake that once belonged to Knox.

His name was Harold Baines, a businessman from Delaware.

At breakfast, Rollie said, "Girls, I have to work today. I'll be gone for six hours or so. Your uncle Bill will be stopping by to check out Buddy. He's thinking of buying a dog. Take him to the dog park, okay?"

"Can he stay for dinner?' Grace said.

"Invite him," Rollie said. "Believe me, he'll stay."

After breakfast, Rollie waited in his office for Teal to arrive. Teal drove up in his unmarked cruiser and parked in front of Grace's car.

"Why didn't you tell me about Clapper's little visit before it happened?" Teal said. "I would have had him picked up for…"

"He never would have come near me if he smelled police," Rollie said. "Besides, I mailed copies of everything to your house, which should get there today. And he doesn't know about the tapes."

"You could have told me this yesterday instead of at six o'clock this morning," Teal said.

"I saved you from a breakfast of carrot sticks," Rollie said. "The girls are keeping a plate of Belgium waffles and bacon warm for you."

"In that case, I forgive you," Teal said. "How long will you be gone?"

"Six hours, give or take."

"Since I haven't had breakfast, lead the way," Teal said.

Rollie and Teal went to the kitchen where the girls greeted Teal with big hugs.

"Sit down, Uncle Bill, and I'll get your breakfast," Grace said.

Teal sat at the table. Giselle poured a glass of orange juice while Grace placed a stack of waffles with bacon in front of him.

"What kind of dog are you looking to get, Uncle Bill?" Gloria said.

Teal looked at Rollie.

"I have to go," Rollie said. "Girls, take it easy on your Uncle Bill."

·　　·　　·

It was one hundred and twenty-five miles to the home of Harold Baines in Wilmington, Delaware.

It was a straight run down 95 South, and Rollie figured he'd be there before noon.

He kept his mind free of thoughts and concentrated on driving. He stopped once for coffee in Pennsylvania and sat at an outside table to drink it.

Harold Baines was a retired businessman, which was all Rollie knew of him.

We'll see where this leads, Rollie thought as he got back in his car. He set the GPS unit again and arrived at Baines's nice home in the Wilmington suburbs sixty-five minutes later.

Baines answered the door when Rollie rang the doorbell. He was close to seventy, thin, and wore rimless glasses.

"Yes?" Baines said.

"Mr. Baines? Harold Baines?" Rollie said.

"Yes. Can I help you?"

Rollie handed his wallet to Baines. "Mr. Baines, this is my New York State private investigator's license."

Rollie handed Baines Teal's business card.

"Before you agree to talk to me, please call police captain William Teal, and verify I am who I say," Rollie said. "I'll wait here."

•   •   •

Mrs. Baines served coffee and cake in the kitchen while Rollie and her husband talked.

"So if I understand you correctly, you and Police Captain Teal want to use my cabin on Big Pond Lake for a stakeout," Baines said. "To catch a man who murdered his wife and buried her in the woods?"

"That's correct, sir," Rollie said.

"I haven't been up there this year," Baines said. "I had open-heart surgery for a blocked artery."

"I'm sorry to hear that," Rollie said.

"I'm fine now, complete recovery," Baines said. "Would you do me a favor?"

"Of course."

"Let me know the condition of the property," Baines said. "I had my boat put in the water in hopes I could spend a few days there."

•   •   •

Teal was taking a nap on the sofa when Rollie walked in the door at 4:30 in the afternoon.

The girls were in the backyard with Buddy.

"Girls, what did you do to your uncle?" Rollie said.

"Played soccer and Frisbee at the dog park," Grace said.

"Come in the house, I need to talk to you," Rollie said.

In the kitchen, Rollie made some fresh coffee. "Go wake Sleeping Beauty," he said.

A few minutes later, Teal stumbled into the kitchen, escorted by the girls. Rollie filled two mugs with coffee and gave one to Teal.

"Everybody grab a seat," Rollie said.

"Is something wrong, Dad?" Grace asked.

"Your Uncle and I are working on a very serious investigation," Rollie said. "We have to go out of town for a few days. As a precaution, we're having two police officers stay with you until we return."

"Dad, what's going on?" Grace said.

"We're investigating a very dangerous man," Rollie said. "Just as a precaution, we want police protection for you in the house."

"Cool," Gloria said.

"Will they be men-cops," Grace asked, "in their early twenties?"

"Afraid not," Teal said. "I need experience for this assignment. They'll be old-timers."

"When?" Grace said.

"Tomorrow morning," Rollie said. "So, we'll need to go to the grocery store before dinner tonight. Grace, you and I will go. Your uncle will stay here with Giselle and Gloria."

"Know any video games?" Gloria said to Teal.

•   •   •

After dinner, Rollie and Teal talked briefly in Rollie's office.

"What time am I picking you up?" Teal said.

"Eight o'clock," Rollie said. "We'll have breakfast here before heading out."

"I'll bring the two officers with me," Teal said.

"See you at 8:00," Rollie said.

"Rollie?" Teal said.

"I know," Rollie said. "Just think of the promotion you'll get when this is all over."

CHAPTER FIFTY-ONE

After breakfast, Rollie showed the two detectives from Teal's precinct his bedroom and the rest of the house.

"Girls, you stay in the yard until we get back," Rollie said.

"What about Buddy?" Gloria said. "He needs his walks."

"Backyard only," Rollie said.

Teal looked at his two detectives. "Unless the house is on fire, they are confined to the house and the backyard," he said.

"Alright, girls, see you in a few days," Rollie said.

•   •   •

"First stop, Manhattan," Rollie said.

"I want to hit that donut shop on 57," Teal said.

"You just had breakfast."

"For the long ride ahead," Teal said.

"It isn't that long."

"Is that tie pin working?" Teal said.

"Receiver and transmitter are working fine," Rollie said. "I checked both this morning."

Teal said there were a pair of twelve-gauges in the trunk, just in case.

Rollie nodded. "Those detectives?" he said.

"Both twenty-year men," Teal said. "I wouldn't have picked them if they weren't top-shelf."

"Good," Rollie said.

Once they reached Manhattan, Teal parked across the street from Knox's headquarters beside a fire hydrant. He tossed his police card on the dashboard to ward off getting a ticket.

"Be back in a few minutes," Rollie said.

"Watch your back," Teal told him.

Rollie crossed the street and entered Knox's very busy headquarters and headed straight for the office.

Karl came out of the crowd and cut Rollie off. "You got some fucking nerve showing your ass around here," Karl said.

"I forgot to tell Knox something from the other night," Rollie said. "It will only take a minute."

"*One* minute," Karl said and opened the office door.

Rollie followed Karl into the office. Knox was behind his desk, reading a document and didn't look up until Karl said, "Look what just walked in."

Knox looked up. "Are you fucking shitting me?" he said.

"I told him," Karl said.

"This will only take a minute," Rollie said.

"Go on," Knox said.

"I checked your website this morning," Rollie said. "You have a fundraiser at the Plaza at 7:30 tonight."

"What of it?" Knox said. "Don't tell me you want a ticket."

Rollie took a chair opposite the desk.

"By all means, have a seat," Knox said.

"When I was eight years old, I had this dog," Rollie said. "A real mutt, but I loved him. He died when I was twelve, and my parents allowed me to bury him in the backyard."

"Is there some point to this little melodrama?" Knox said.

"I'm getting to it," Rollie said. "So anyway, I dug a hole three feet deep and buried my dog in the backyard. And do you know what happened?"

"Finch, get to the point," Knox said.

"About three years later, a sinkhole developed where I had buried the dog," Rollie said. "See, without a coffin, once the dog decomposed, the ground on top of him collapsed and created a sinkhole."

"What the fuck does...?" Knox said, pausing and glaring at Rollie.

"That's right," Rollie said. "A sinkhole. And right now, I'm off to Delaware County to ask a judge for a warrant to have deputies search the woods for a sinkhole, and when we find it, what do you think we're going to dig up? My guess is the first Mrs. Knox."

"No judge will grant you a warrant for that," Knox said.

"We shall see," Rollie said and stood up.

Karl blocked the door.

"My tie pin is a transmitter to the police right outside," Rollie said. "Captain, ring my cell phone."

Rollie's cell phone immediately rang.

"Excuse me, Karl, you're in my way," Rollie said. "Oh, and some very capable police officers are staying at my house to watch my girls, just in case Karl decides to get stupid again."

•　　•　　•

"That went well," Teal said as he ate a donut. "By now, Knox is on his way to those woods."

"He's not going anywhere until after that fundraiser," Rollie said. "He figures we won't be able to get a warrant for a few days, so he'll think it through and take his time. After the fundraiser is over, he'll drive to the woods and lead us straight to the body."

"Are you sure about that?" Teal said.

"I saw it in his eyes when he realized what my dog story was about," Rollie said.

"Is that story true, by the way?" Teal said.

"Every word."

"We're about thirty minutes from the cabin," Teal said. "They got a grocery store in that hick-town?"

CHAPTER FIFTY-TWO

After stopping at a small grocery store in town, Teal drove to the cabin and parked behind it where the car couldn't be seen from the road.

"We have plenty of time," Rollie said. "I'm going to take a nap."

"A nap?" Teal said.

"It's going to be a late night," Rollie said.

"How do you figure?" Teal said.

"His fundraiser is scheduled to and at 10:30," Rollie said. "Say, an hour to gather everything you need and then hit the road. That puts him here around 1:30 in the morning, possibly closer to 2:00."

"Maybe I'll grab a nap, too," Teal said.

•　•　•

Rollie woke up at 6:00 p.m. and made a pot of coffee. The aroma woke Teal, and Rollie filled two large mugs.

They sat at the kitchen table.

"We should think about some dinner," Teal said. "We got two pizzas and a bucket of chicken, which do you prefer?"

"Let's do the chicken," Rollie said. "Knowing you, you'll probably want a pizza around ten o'clock."

"Like you said, a long night," Teal said.

Rollie got the large bucket of chicken from the fridge. Included was a bowl of mashed potatoes, six biscuits, and a small chocolate cake.

Rollie nuked the chicken and potatoes in the microwave and called home while the food heated.

"Hi, Dad," Grace said.

"Everything okay?" Rollie said.

"Fine. We made the detectives lasagna for dinner," Grace said. "And that three-step ice cream in a jar for dessert."

"Okay," Rollie said. "In bed by 10:00, and listen to the detectives."

"We will. Promise," Grace said.

Rollie hung up and brought the chicken, mashed potatoes, and biscuits to the table.

"There's nothing like a hot bucket of chicken," Teal said.

As he bit into a leg, Teal said, "Have you given any thought to the Assistant Chief of D's offer? Andrews isn't going to wait forever."

"Actually, I have been thinking about it," Rollie said. "Mostly because of Knox. I can't expose my girls to that kind of danger anymore. It's a nice job with a good salary, and Grace turns eighteen in a few weeks and has her own car now, so I think I'm going to say yes, if Andrews will still have me."

"Glad to have you back on the job, Rollie," Teal said.

After eating, Rollie made more coffee, and they took mugs outside and sat on the bench in front of the house to watch the sun set over the lake.

"Living in the city makes you forget sights like this," Teal said.

"Living in the city makes you forget a lot of things," Rollie said.

They watched the sun go down and then went back inside the cabin.

"Now comes the hard part, the waiting," Teal said.

Rollie drew all curtains and drapes and kept just the kitchen light on. He opened his briefcase and took out several long candles. He set the candles on the table and lit them with a match, then turned the lights off.

"I brought a deck of cards," Rollie said.

They played for several hours until Teal said, "My eyes are killing me, these damn candles."

"It's ten o'clock," Rollie said.

"And I'm ready for a snack," Teal said.

Teal heated a pizza in the oven. When it was hot, he placed it on the table and cut it into slices.

"What did you tell the Delaware County Sheriff's Department?" Rollie said.

"I'd call thirty minutes after Knox arrived," Teal said. "But I'm rethinking that."

"Don't," Rollie said. "We want Knox to have enough time to lead us to the body, or we're here for nothing."

Teal nodded as he put a slice of pizza on a plate for Rollie and then for himself.

"This is the part of the job I always hated," Teal said. "The waiting. I never minded kicking in doors, but the waiting always gets to me."

"Play some more cards?" Rollie said.

"Why not?" Teal said.

They played until midnight.

"Is he going to show," Teal said.

"He'll show," Rollie said. "He can't take the chance and call my bluff."

Teal went to the kitchen window, which faced the woods across the street, and looked out.

"Good moon," he said.

"That's all we'll need," Rollie said.

"Yeah, and some luck," Teal said.

. . .

Drinking a mug of coffee, Rollie kept watch at the kitchen window. Teal sat at the table, also with a full mug.

At 1:45, the lights of Knox's SUV lit up the dark road.

"Bill, blow out that candle and come over here," Rollie said.

Teal blew out the one candle still burning and stood beside Rollie.

Knox, Karl, and two additional men exited the SUV. They carried shovels and flashlights.

Knox and the two additional men walked into the woods. Karl kept watch beside the SUV.

"As they say on Broadway," Teal said, " it's show time."

Rollie had a small flashlight and he used it to open his briefcase. He removed his .357 Magnum revolver and several speed loaders. He put the revolver in his belt and the speed loaders in his right pants pocket.

He also removed a retractable baton that, with a flick of the wrist, telescoped from eight to eighteen inches. The tip was a steel ball. The handle had a leather strap.

Last, Rollie removed a pair of brass knuckles.

"Karl is mine," Rollie said.

"Let's go then," Teal said.

They left the cabin, and Teal brought the shotguns.

Behind them, the moon glistened on the lake.

"A beautiful sight," Teal whispered.

"By the time he sees us, it will be too late to react," Rollie whispered. "Ready?"

"Yeah."

They walked up the dirt driveway to the street, which was about twelve feet wide.

Karl was leaning against the SUV, smoking a cigarette.

"You gotta be fucking kidding me," Karl said when, all of a sudden, Rollie raced across the road with the baton in his right hand.

Karl reached for his Glock.

Rollie flicked his wrist, extended the baton, and cracked Karl across his right hand before he could draw his gun.

Stunned, Karl didn't react. Rollie smacked him across the jaw with the baton, and Karl crashed into the SUV. Then Rollie grabbed Karl's Glock and tossed it to Teal. Rollie compressed the baton, put it into his pocket, and slid the brass knuckles onto his right hand.

Rollie turned Karl around. "For my daughters," he said, and punched Karl three times in the stomach with the brass knuckles.

Karl fell to his knees and gasped loudly for air.

"And this is for me," Rollie said and he punched Karl in the jaw, knocking him unconscious.

"Cuff him," Rollie said. "We'll throw him in the SUV."

"Do your daughters know what a savage you are?" Teal said.

They tossed Karl into the back seat of the SUV.

"Give the Delaware Sheriff a call," Rollie said.

Teal called it in and turned to Rollie. "Twenty minutes, tops," he said.

"Let's go," Rollie said.

Rollie took off into the woods and followed the makeshift path.

After about a hundred and fifty feet, Rollie stopped. "See that?" he whispered.

About seventy-five yards northwest, a bright lantern lit up the woods.

"Yeah," Teal whispered.

"Let's go, and be quiet," Rollie whispered.

They made their way slowly through the woods until they could hear Knox speaking.

"Come on guys, put your backs into it," Knox said.

"How fucking deep did you bury her?" one of the men said.

"Deep enough," Knox said.

Rollie and Teal continued walking until they were ten feet from Knox.

"That's enough digging fellows," Rollie said.

The two men digging dropped their shovels, and one of them produced a handgun.

Rollie shot him in the chest. "That wasn't very smart," Rollie said. "Bill, cover the other one."

Teal stepped forward with the shotgun aimed at the second man. "Be smart and stay in that hole," he said.

"There's a dead man in here," the man said.

"They'll be two dead men in there if you move," Teal said.

Rollie walked to Knox. "Got you," Rollie said.

"How much? Name your price," Knox said.

"Priceless," Rollie said. "Seeing you on every cable news show is priceless. Just like my daughters are."

"Rollie, please," Knox begged.

Off in the distance, police sirens sounded.

"That's your ride, Knox," Rollie said.

"I'm begging you," Knox said.

"You know that story you told me about the alpha wolf, well, I'm not a wolf and I never submit," Rollie said.

ABOUT THE AUTHOR

Al Lamanda is a native of New York City. In addition to his many mysteries, he also writes Western novels under the name Ethan J. Wolfe. He has been nominated for many awards, and won the Nero Wolfe Award for Best Mystery of the Year for his novel, *With 6 You Get Wally,* book five in the John Bekker Mysteries. The series continues with *Who Killed Joe Italiano?* (Encircle Publications, 2018), and *For Deader or Worse* (Encircle Publications, 2019). His latest stand-alone novel, *City of Darkness,* was published by Encircle in January, 2021. Al is always working on his next novel. Watch for more titles—including John Bekker #8—coming soon!

If you enjoyed reading this book,
please consider writing your honest review
and sharing it with other readers.

Many of our Authors are happy to participate in
Book Club and Reader Group discussions.
For more information, contact us at info@encirclepub.com.

Thank you,
Encircle Publications

For news about more exciting new fiction, join us at:

Facebook: www.facebook.com/encirclepub

Twitter: twitter.com/encirclepub

Instagram: www.instagram.com/encirclepublications

Sign up for Encircle Publications newsletter and specials:
eepurl.com/cs8taP

www.ingramcontent.com/pod-product-compliance
Lightning Source LLC
Chambersburg PA
CBHW020615110726
47899CB00002B/514